Truths become lies, and lies become truths when veiled in dark magic.

This isn't your mother's sweet love story and it's not your sister's fairytale. Pedalstem Lillies is dark, dangerous, and highly addictive. You will share in every experience the hero and heroine have, as their quest for the truth leads them to the hateful dark void that threatens to consume their souls

Chaos Unleashed
Copyright © 2012 AmBear Shellea
ISBN: 978-1-77111-291-8
Cover art by Angela Waters

Published by Devine Destinies
An imprint of eXtasy Books
Look for us online at:
www.devinedestinies.com

Chaos Unleashed Pedalstem Lillies

By

AmBear Shellea

Thank you, God, for giving me the ability and determination to fulfill my dream, and my friends and family for their valued support, and not letting me give up when I got frustrated. All the "writer friends" I have made, that have helped to turn light on and point me in the right direction. Without all of you, this dream would still just be floating round in my head, and not the reality it has become. A big Thank you, to Devine Destinies/ecstasy books, for giving me the opportunity to share my wild and crazy fantasy with the world.

Prologue

Run! Her instincts urged her farther, faster, deeper into the woods. Trees passed at record speed in her peripheral vision as she ran for safety. Red chanced a look behind her, the hunters quickly closing in, faces unrecognizable, and intentions unknown.

Branches snatched at her clothes and hair, as if the hands of her pursuers. Breathing heavily, her chest constricted, her lungs on fire, and still she fled. Her fast beating heart pounded in her ears. *Almost there.* Her home, in view, meant protection and help. Drenched in sweat, her dress clung to her frame and hindered her movements.

Faster! The sound of crunching leaves and snapping twigs told her they were right on her heels. Her gaze frantically swept the area looking for her knight in peasant clothes. Two against three were better odds. The shadows darting between the trees gave away the hunters' position. Three men, still in pursuit a few feet away, but Woody was nowhere to be seen. Then she heard him.

"Red, run!"

Heart pounding, she stopped, turning in the direction of his voice. She could see no sign of him and she no longer heard his voice. *Oh, no...they must have captured him.* Gripped in fear, she turned to bolt once more, only to trip and collide with the moss-covered tree. For a split second her body stuck to the bark. Her arms wrapped around the trunk, she dropped to the ground.

Falling! Air exploded from her lungs and her muscles tightened as her slender frame slammed onto the hard earth. Searing pain ran through her. Salty tears stung her eyes and she could feel a lump already forming where her head had struck a sharp rock.

The light of the setting sun dimmed slowly as if someone were turning down the wick of an oil lamp. The flame colored sky, olive green leaves, and bright red tree blossoms slowly drained of all their color, leaving only different shades of gray. She blinked her eyes and tried to fend off the tunnel vision closing in. Unconsciousness reached a welcoming hand her way. Non-responsive muscles made it impossible to move. Feet still trampling through the underbrush echoed in her ears.

She clenched her jaw and closed her eyes as she tried to push her body from the ground. It had no effect. Her muscles were tightly locked and stiff. She could feel her body, and the grass beneath her skin, but she couldn't lift a finger, limbs frozen in place by an unknown force. Paralysis or something else, she didn't know.

No color around her, Red felt a spider web of numbness spread through her limbs and she knew it was over. She had lost. *If this is how it's to end, I must see it.*

Staring into the darkening sky, she viewed the scene in horror and wonder. Her world, in black and white, blurred and spun slowly. The haze of the vortex swirled above, closing in, and extinguishing what was left of the light from the sky. Stars twisting and twirling with the clouds and the moon, as if in a mixing bowl of chaos. *I can't...hold on...much longer. I hope he's close enough to hear my last words.* Darkness pressed in harder and harder and she parted her lips to speak.

"Always know, even in the grip of death, your Lady Red loves you."

She felt the cold arms of darkness engulf her and madness take over her mind. Her ears played his voice one last time as she slipped away.

"No! Fight it. Please don't leave me. I need you, I love you!"

Chapter One
A Fight for Freedom

A muffled noise sounded in her ear, a man's voice. Her head lolled from side to side as she worked through the fog in her mind. Her eyes fluttered softly as she tried to awaken. The side of her skull throbbed with a dull pain. Placing her hand behind her ear, she found the source, a small gash. *What happened?* Blaze scanned her surroundings through her hazy vision. *How did I get here? How did I get hurt?* She felt disoriented and confused.

The voice spoke again, sounding urgent. She focused on the accent, and the haze slowly cleared. Her eyes narrowed as a distorted figure appeared. *Friend or foe?* He was an older man with dark eyes and a fierce expression.

"Who are you? What do you want?"

Her elbows dug into the earth and she crawled backwards quickly. Fear had her fully awake and in survival mode. Her mind blew the fog and haze away, like a swift breeze, leaving her clear headed and on alert.

"Get the ropes, boys. She'll need to be bound for the trip."

Ropes? Trip? I have to get out of here. Rolling onto her knees, she jumped from the ground and attempted to run. Halfway up and two steps away she dropped, face planting into the grass.

"Get off me!"

Blaze thrashed along the ground as she tried to throw him off. Firm hands grabbed her arms and jerked them behind her. She bit her lip to keep from crying out. A coarse rope burned her wrists when the man forcefully tied them together.

"Why are you doing this? Please. Please…let me go."

She felt his knee in her back. Pain ran the length of her spine as the man leaned over. Her nostrils flared, her mouth watered, and her stomach churned as the foul stench of booze and body odor filled her nose.

"No need to worry, lass. We are just going on a little trip."

She pulled air back in her lungs as the man got up and walked away. Looking in the direction of his movements, she noticed he stopped a few feet away and spoke to two others.

"Get her into the wagon with the other prisoner."

Tears dripped from her cheeks and she trembled in fear. She watched in horror as the pair walked in her direction, two young boys, tall and lean, sporting shaggy sand-colored hair. Medium builds covered in traveling clothes and heavy boots carried them closer. Baby faces with muddy eyes glared back at her. Two deep breaths escaped her lungs and they were upon her.

"No! No! No! Please, no."

Blaze brought her boots up and kicked wildly at the hands reaching for her. Pinning her feet to the ground, they rolled her over and pulled her up by the arms. Pain coursed through her bound limbs, forcing her to put weight on wobbly legs. Now, standing upright, they urged her to move. Her feet stumbled slightly as she walked to the wooden farm cart. She blinked away her watery-eyed vision and spotted the wagon with the other prisoner.

Where are they taking me? What did I do to deserve this?

She jerked and pulled as she fought for freedom. Her elbow made contact and she dug into the boy's side. She turned to run. A strong hand grabbed her firmly and whirled her around. Her eyes and the boy's eyes met at the last second before her world spun and she crashed onto the ground.

Head throbbing in pace with the beating of her heart, facial skin and muscles on fire, she realized what happened. Tears of anguish and fury filled her already stinging eyes. She knew the pain might send her into unconsciousness, but she slightly moved her jaw and tested for breakage. Blackness threatened to suck her in. Her eyes almost viewed the back of her skull and she fought to stay awake. *Not broken.* Blaze shook her head slightly and tried to clear away the colorful dancing stars. Her face pressed into the side of her shoulder as she attempted to rub the sting away. *That was a slap? It felt like he used his fist.*

The two young men picked her up and roughly heaved her into the wagon. Pulling her knees to her side, she dropped her head in defeat. *Are they going to kill me? I don't want to die.* Her body shook with uncontrollable sobs. Dirt and grass smeared the front of her tear-soaked dress. Heat and electricity shot through her when a thumb caressed the side of her hand. Her body stiffened at the unexpected touch.

The other prisoner.

His soft voice sounded behind her.

"Are you okay?"

"No…" she sniffled and cleared her throat.

"What happened? Why have they captured you?"

"I don't know."

Her wrists, scraped and burned, felt on fire as she pulled them this way and that, testing the strength of the ropes. Survival instincts refused to leave and optimism urged her to try. With her eyes closed, she lowered her head and mentally concentrated on her bindings. She stretched her fingers and pulled on the line as she worked to loosen the knots. Hope whispered she could do it while the dark voice of despair told her hope was a liar.

The stranger sounded in her ear along with a warm touch on her hand. "Here, let me get closer. Perhaps we can help each other."

Blaze could feel his strong back against hers. The heat radiated from him, soothing her aching muscles as though wrapped in a warm blanket. *That feels nice.* She opened her eyes, lifted her head, and checked on her captors. Three huddled bodies sat upon the front seat in deep conversation. Blaze heard whispered words exchanged in haste, but couldn't make out what they were saying. Only two names, Benjamin and Bernard—the young boys. Loud yelling filled the air followed by the slapping of reins. Her shoulder banged against the wood, landing her on her side, as the wagon lurched forward. Struggling a bit, she used her elbows and worked herself back into the sitting position. Another question muttered from behind as he pressed against her once more.

"What is your name? Mine is Demarko."

"Blaze. My name is Blaze. "

The twisting and pulling caused more burns, but it finally paid off. *Yes!* She pulled her arms forward to rub the fire out of them. *The ropes are off, now how to get away?*

"Any ideas on our next move?" She kept her voice quiet.

"I'm thinking about that. Give me a second."

Wheels spun in her head as she sifted through worst case scenarios. Jumping from the moving wagon and making a run for it seemed a *doomed from the start* kind of plan. His soft voice tickled her wet skin.

"I have an idea, but I'm not sure it's a good one."

"Let's hear it."

"They are not paying attention, so that'll give us an advantage."

"Advantage for what?" Blaze turned in his direction. "What exactly is your plan?"

"I'm not sure it will work, but it's worth a try. I don't know where they are taking us, but by their actions, I know we don't want to go."

"And…"

"I say we push those three out of the wagon and move those horses, as well as ourselves, away from here until we figure out what's going on."

"Why not? It's better than what I came up with. My plan was to jump and make a run for it. I like our chances with your idea."

"I just hope it works."

It was a bad plan created out of desperation. *All or nothing.* She checked on her abductors. They were still engrossed in their own conversation and paid attention to little else. Palms flat on the wagon, she crept onto her toes. *Wonderful! No one noticed.*

Blaze followed Demarko's lead. *Dear God, please let this work.* Facing the front in a crouching position, she glanced at the man next to her. Silently, she counted his breaths and waited for

Demarko's signal. *Now!* They flung themselves at the three in the front of them.

She flew through the air arms out and knocked Bernard sprawling onto the ground next to the pounding hooves of the horses. She watched his body drop. Quickly, he rolled to the side out of trampling distance. *Dammit, he was quick. What a shame.* Giddiness and hope set in as it looked as though this plan might work. She seemed quite pleased when she turned her head and saw Demarko in action. His frame went airborne as he positioned his hands to hit the men in the center of their backs. When he made contact, the big man fell out of the wagon and landed on the ground. Benjamin then leapt on one of the galloping horses. She and Demarko tried to regain and maintain their balance as the wagon raced onward. Benjamin kept a death grip on the horse's neck. Smiling, she watched as the boy flashed a look of horror on his face.

Bernard and the big man got off the ground intent on chasing the wagon and its escaping prisoners.

Hands on the wooden seat, Blaze worked with Demarko and reached for the reins that flapped against the dirt. She wanted to laugh aloud at the boy on the horse. He almost lost his balance, but to her surprise, Benjamin maneuvered himself onto his back. Careful not to fall, he grabbed the horse's middle with both legs and leaned forward quickly.

"Stop!" she heard from behind her.

It was obvious by the still escaping horses that his outburst didn't have the desired effect. A comment on her lips soon cut off as the man whistled. Her body hit the dirt path hard, followed by Demarko and Benjamin, as the horses halted abruptly. Blaze jumped from the ground and rushed to the wagon intent on escape. Another electric current pulsed beneath her skin as Demarko's hand covered hers when they both reached for the reins. Her waist was encircled in his strong arms as he hoisted her into the wagon. She scooted over quickly, making room for him as he jumped in, reins in hand. She grasped the wooden seat tightly. *Ouch! Splinters!* Demarko slapped the reins, leaving the terrorizing trio in a cloud of dust. Squinting her eyes due to the dirt and wind, she watched the three men stop running and stare as their captives got away.

"We did it!" Her body filled with the warmth of joy and hope. She wrapped her arms around his neck. "Your plan worked."

"I wasn't sure it would, but it was the only chance we had."

"Thank God it worked. I'm glad to be away from them."

"Why did they capture you in the first place? I mean, what did you do?"

Blaze pulled away and folded her hands in her lap. "I don't know. I have no idea who they are or why I was being taken."

"What *do* you remember?"

She placed her hand on her chin and plunged into her mind for the answer. Her eyes widened and her body stiffened. She broke out in a cold sweat. Her hand tangled in her hair and her body shook, as she looked at Demarko when he spoke.

"That's what I thought."

"What happened? What did they do to me?"

Ragged breaths pulled through her lungs, heart rate picked up pace, and she slowly slipped into the void of her mind. *What happened? Why can't I remember anything? My mind is…blank. No, not my mind…my memories. No clues, no answers, just deep dark nothingness. How can this be? How's this even possible?* Tiny stinging needles, all at once, seem to stab into her brain, as she plunged deeper into her subconscious. She spiraled further into panic and Demarko's voice sent the life preserver that kept her from completely drowning.

"Let me guess…nothing?"

"Wait. How did you—"

"Know? I know because my memories are gone, too. I wondered, well, hoped, maybe you would know something. By your reactions it wasn't hard to figure out."

"Are you saying they have done something, not stress induced? How is that possible? How do you steal someone's memories?"

"I don't have any idea. As to whether or not *they* did something…maybe. They looked to be capable of anything."

Sobs overtook her as the realization of what that meant sank in. *I don't know who I am. What am I to do? Where do I go? Where is my home? Can I be safe not knowing whom I can and can't trust?*

Diamond-sized tears dropped from her cheeks. She let Demarko pull her close when he reached for her. She soaked the side of his shirt as she let the events of the day pour out completely. Blaze took the pain, fear, shock, and despair, and roped them together pulling them forward. One by one, she let them go. Each emotional departure left her body and she felt a little lighter. She coaxed her breathing to even out and mentally pictured her heart rate slowing while she searched for the calm within. Relaxation finally took hold and her eyes drooped as she lost the fight to stay awake. Green grass, a light breeze, and the sun's rays dancing like fairies along her skin filled her dream.

Her body shook slightly followed by Demarko's voice as he woke her from a peaceful slumber.

"Blaze, wake up."

With her hands on his side, she pushed herself into an upright position. She wiped the drool from her mouth and the matted dust from her eyes. Swallowing past the grime in her throat, she noticed the scenery was stationary.

"Why are we stopped?"

"We need water and so do the horses. They are lathered from all the running. I think we have put enough distance between us and them to rest a minute."

"Water sounds wonderful. I'm parched from all of this dust."

Stiff and sore legs protested her movements as she stood. Her muscles almost groaned in relief when she forced them to stretch. *Oh, that feels good.* Strong arms engulfed her when her foot slid off the wagon. Heat lingered just under the surface. With his help, she righted herself and steadied her footing. The air from his lungs tickled her ear as he spoke.

"Let me help you down."

Her eyes watched his movements. He jumped from the wagon and turned back to her in one swift motion. Extending his arm, he reached up for her. Placing her hand in his, she carefully climbed out of the wagon.

"Thank You."

Crickets sounded off, leaves rustled in the wind, and shadows played between the trees as moonlight blanketed the area. Chills trailed the length of her spine as an eerie feeling crept along her skin. She knew its cause. The clear open area left them exposed and at risk for being caught. Slowly she turned in a complete circle and glanced around. To her left grew tall trees with low hanging, full branches. The trunks grew wide and close together. To the right was the rough dirt road and open area. Her ears heard the most glorious sound, the tune of a soft trickling stream off in the distance. The smile slid off her face and was replaced by confusion when she glanced in Demarko's direction.

"What are you doing? Don't we need them attached to that wagon to get away?"

"No. We can gain ground quicker on horseback. I don't think the wagon is going to do very well beyond those trees. We can walk the horses down to the water. Once they have rested and gotten a drink we'll head out again. We need to keep moving."

"Well, that makes sense." Goosebumps all over, she tried to rub the uneasy feeling away while she watched him work.

His hands moved quickly and it didn't take long before the horses were free of their bindings. Surprised, she noticed him walking toward her. She saw his eyes take in the features of her face. By the anger hardening the color of his pupils, she knew what he saw. Trying not to wince at the sting still upon her cheek, she closed her eyes when he caressed the handprint she felt still there. It only lasted a moment. Heat and electricity fused together and swam in her veins when he touched her. She reveled in it. Electric shock waves soared from head to toe and back. Her body felt light as air. Her knees weakened and her head threatened to float away. The feeling stopped when she felt him remove his hand and ask her a question. Opening her eyes, she looked at him.

"Are you in pain?"

She cleared her throat and answered, "I'm fine. It only stings a little now." *Do I know him? He seems familiar. Maybe he's just a kind man, but...*

Her mind raced onward at lightning speed as she studied the raw emotion in his face. His eyes were full of thoughtfulness and care that equally matched the touch he left on her cheek. She never wanted him to move, but he did. However, the warmth she felt on her face, she now felt all over. Reins in one hand, his hand in the other, they walked into the woods.

Knees bent underneath her, she filled her hands with water and drank from the stream. *Refreshing and revitalizing.* Just the simple act of drinking water made her whole body come alive as it washed away the dirt and dust that had collected there. Her eyes focused and she took in the serene scene.

The stream looked so inviting after the dirt-filled day. It flowed gently across the moss-covered rocks as if to say come join me. Trickling downward, the stream grew bigger and deeper. The moonlight bounced and played among the soft ripples. It was magnificent. *I wonder if we have enough time to enjoy this. A few minutes shouldn't hurt. After all, we have ridden for hours and the confounded comrades are on foot.*

Dress in hand, she slid her bare feet into the cool stream and delighted in the fresh feeling. She looked at Demarko as he watered the horses, paying no attention to her. She bent over, cupped her hands in the water, and sent small waves in his direction. He turned her way and gave her a coy smile. *What a charming smile.* He let go of the horses and bent down, splashing her back. Caught up in splashing enthusiastically and unaware of his whereabouts, she suddenly saw him appear next to her. It took her by surprise when he grabbed her. Stuck in his embrace, she felt him pull her out into deeper water. Blaze squirmed and twisted in his arms as she tried half-heartedly to get away. Laughter played in her voice when he pulled them under. She sprang up like a daisy in a field, still in his grip and wiped the liquid out of her eyes.

There's that feeling again. It's better than before. Heat and electricity mixed with the coolness of the water. Heaven! Her pulse was equal to the beating of a war drum against her neck, and her body felt as if it might explode from the inside out. She knew he felt it, too, from the look on his face and the feel of his body. *I could get addicted to this.* She let the present fill her ears.

Laughter echoed through the trees. It promised to be a new day. She giggled when she heard the horses neigh as if they were laughing also. However, freedom would be short lived if they stayed too long. She let him help her onto the bank.

"That was fun. I feel better. How about you?"

"Yes. I do feel better...and cleaner. Guess if you are going to wash dust and dirt off, that's the best way." She wrung the water from her dress.

"I'll see if I can get a fire going so we can dry our clothes."

Her eyes on his figure, she watched him until he disappeared into the woods. His precise and quick movements suggested he spent a lot of time in the wilderness. It wasn't long before he reappeared with an armload of small branches and dropped it on the ground.

"I think I'll go tend to the horses so we can leave soon." Turning her back to him, she wandered over to the horses. They looked to be feeling better and were eating grass when she found them. She held both the reins and led them to a nearby tree. "Easy now."

She fastened them to the tree and looked for a small branch among the forest debris littered about. *That looks like a good one right there.* Stick in hand, she moved it down the horse's mane and continued the rest of their bodies. Her hands moved in circular motions as she removed all the dirt and grass from the animals. While her hand was between the mare's ears, the horse nudged her back in kind.

"Doesn't that feel better?"

Lighter than air, she felt she could live here forever. It was beautiful and peaceful. Her mind filled with images of the way he looked at her. The smile on his face held tenderness, compassion, and when they touched, it was electrifying. *If only my memories would come back then I would know who I am and maybe who he is.* She couldn't explain it. Somehow, she felt she knew him, but the sensation kept fading too quickly. Blackness would surround it and cause it to slip through her delicate fingers as small grains of beach sand.

Finished with the horses and with reins redone, she noticed the glow from small flames. She double checked that the horses were secured tightly and unable to flee, then ambled over and stood by the fire. Just as the cool water felt refreshing, the warmth from the fire was just as delightful.

"I will be right back. I'm going to gather some larger logs for the fire."

"Okay." She turned in the direction of his voice, but he vanished once again.

* * * *

Weaving in and out of trees, arms filled with tinder, Demarko walked back toward the fire. Just beyond the trees, he spotted her and stopped. She filled his line of vision, just standing there drying her hair. She was so beautiful. Her cream-colored skin contrasted with her bright fiery red hair hanging in soft spirals. Her frame looked frail as her chest lifted with each breath. Her movements were graceful. *How can she even move in that dress? It fits her figure like a second skin. It must be the slits up the side…they are ripped to her hips. Look at those legs…wow!* His eyes traced the curves of her shapely figure. *That plain brown dress is torn and dirty, yet, somehow, she looks like royalty.*

He marveled at her, all of her, not just her beauty. She had exhibited bravery and even toughness. She was scared and yet not afraid to fight for herself. *Brave and gorgeous: a lethal combination.* He knew with certainty she was the most beautiful woman he had ever seen. Amazement grabbed hold at an odd and seemingly unfamiliar sensation. As he looked at her, his face reddened when he realized somehow—and he couldn't figure out how—but he knew her. It seemed almost intimate. Being next to her felt like home.

His body ached for her touch and he craved that feeling of electricity when he touched her. Diving into his mind, he searched his memory for any sign of her. A lush green meadow with trees almost reaching the sky, and a large silver and gray rock formation surrounding a steaming hot spring was all his memory held. He could almost feel the heat from the steam dance across his skin when he thought about it. Demarko glanced back at her and was taken back to see her staring straight at him. *Fiery red hair and sparkling dark green eyes...* To look into those vibrant gems seemed to somehow warm his soul. *If only...*

* * * *

Stuck in the stare of his bright Topaz eyes, Blaze felt as if her heart might burst through her chest in delightful pleasure, and she didn't know why. His eyes were his best feature. They dazzled brightly in the moonlight and yet pierced the soul at the same time. *Beautiful and dangerous.* She felt positive she knew him. She just couldn't remember from where. Standing a few feet taller than her, he seemed of average height. *He is very handsome. Just look at all those muscles stretching that shirt.* His tanned skin gave his sharp features a gentle soft glow when the light moved across his face. Chocolate-colored hair played around his shoulders in soft waves. His light green button front shirt hung open slightly baiting the eye with a small peek at the firm lines on his chest. Khaki colored pants hung off his hips with only a small piece of fabric holding them in place...*my memories would return.*

Her eyes caught in his captivating stare for what seemed like an eternity before he finally broke eye contact and looked away. He walked over and dropped more logs on the fire. She asked a question in hopes of moving past the awkward moment.

"What do you think we should do now?"

"Well, the sun will be up soon. I think we should keep moving. I'm hoping there is a town close by."

"Yes, a town would be great. We could get some food and a good night's rest." She absent mindedly watched the flames of the fire flicker in the breeze.

"Food and a soft bed sound very nice."

"You mentioned your mind was having complications, too?"

"Yes. It's so strange. Knowing my own name came easy enough, but anything else...I don't understand it."

Sliding her hands through her hair, she tried to work out some of the tangles as they talked. "I know how you feel. I think I get close, but it just slips through my fingers. It's so frustrating and exhausting. Makes my head feel as if it's going to explode and stop all together. I don't know... Did you recognize those men?"

"No. I don't know who they are, although I spotted something about the boy named Benjamin. I can't place it, but he is...well...different."

"Now that you mention it, he did have an unusual sparkle to eyes. Did you happen to catch the older man's name?"

"No, he was careful. I noticed Bernard was going to address him, but the big man gave him a stern look. I paid attention only because of how odd it was. I think he might be their father, though. He acted as if that could be the case."

Her pulse picked up as anger filled her body. She felt restless and forlorn. She had to move, so she paced back and forth.

"That's what I guessed as well. I just don't understand any of this. Why the secrecy? It's not as if we *know* anyone. Our memories are gone...wiped clean away. I would love to know what happened. They obviously know. Even if we did know something, who are we going to tell?"

"You want to go back and ask?"

"Yes. I think I do." She watched his face and waited for his reaction.

"What?" he asked with surprise, giving her a strange look. "I was only joking."

"We just got away, so, no, I don't want to go back." She tried to keep the smile from her face, but it just wouldn't stay hidden. Demarko joined in and they both laughed.

Clothes dried and her spirit soaring around her, Blaze felt much better. Snuggled next to Demarko's side, they sat and watched the sunrise. It was peaceful and quiet, but now it came time to go. She walked over, untied the horses, and took them to him while he put out the fire.

"I'm ready to get out of here. I'm starting to get an uneasy feeling."

"Me, too. Just about got the fire put out and then we can go. I say we keep going east until we find a town or something."

"That's a great idea. I'm not sure how long my adrenaline can keep me going before I fall asleep. I hope the town's close."

"Do you need me to help you onto the horse?"

"No, there is a small stump over here I can use to stand on."

With one foot on the stump and the other half over the horse she froze. *That's odd. What's that sound?* Before she could ponder any further, she heard his loud booming voice behind the trees. *They found us!*

"Get them!"

Her eyes scanning the area, she saw the father and Bernard crash into Demarko, knocking him to the ground flat on his back.

Demarko tried to push the two men away. Jumping from the log, she raced over and grabbed Bernard by his hair and collar in an attempt to pull him off. She caused him to lose his grip and he fell, landing atop of her and knocking the wind from her lungs. Knees bent to her chest, she heaved the boy onto the dirt. Bernard landed on his side and tried to get up. She kicked him in the face when his charge brought him close. Like a hunter stalking prey, she eyed him as he held his bloody face in pain. *He's down for a minute. Hard to see with blood in your eyes.* She turned toward Demarko and the other man.

The big man put his hand on Demarko's chest, pulled back and aimed, using Demarko's face as his intended target. Demarko quickly ducked his head to the side, which caused the man to miss by mere inches. Both hands on the man's chest, he placed his boot in the man's gut and hurled him into the air. Both men were now on their feet and braced for anything, glaring at each other trying to anticipate the other's next move. As Blaze stared at Demarko, she could almost taste freedom as the battle leaned in their favor.

There's that sound again—what's that? A soft whisper echoed in her ears and sent the scene before her into bright confusion. She went from intently focused on the enemy to a burning brightness that closing her eyelids couldn't fade. Face hidden in her hands, she cried out in stunned confusion. Her fingers twitched, itching to claw the eyes from her skull. She felt pain so intense, it seemed as if thorns were embedded in her eye sockets. Vines born of violence and rage felt as if they covered her body trapping her in a cocoon of torment. Demarko's excruciating yell followed.

The air went still, the noise ceased, and the bright enemy vanished. Her muscles ached with the effects of the after burn. She panted, trying to catch her breath. Her body lay limp on the grass. She blinked away agonizing tears and worked to clear her vision. No sounds penetrated her ears and no hands grabbed for her. She dared a look around. Her head lifted and she took in the scene.

Her eyes scanned the area and revealed Bernard standing next to her. The big man stood glaring down at Demarko, who lay flat on his back, immobile, as if dead. A small patch of blood matted his hair. Emotion took over logic. She got up and raced to him. When she reached his body, she dropped to her knees beside him as tears trailed down her cheeks. *Dear God, please let him be okay. It's all my fault. We stayed too long.* Her hand cupped his face as she leaned down and pressed her ear to his chest.

"Thank God" she cried out with joy at the sound of his strong beating heart. Blaze couldn't help but smile as she stared at him smiling back at her.

The abductors pushing her aside and took charge of the situation. Cornered and scared, she scratched and clawed wildly at the hands reaching for her. She used all of her strength and tried to break free. It was no use. Strong hands held her in a tight grip while the big man pinned Demarko by placing a boot on his throat. The reality of it hit home and she knew her freedom was gone. Fatigue and terror had her muscles trembling as she prepared for the worst. Her thoughts, running a hundred miles an hour and all over the place, stopped suddenly when the man spoke. She looked him in the face. *He has an evil smile.*

"Lady, you will cooperate, or I'll crush his windpipe."

Her gaze followed his movements as he applied pressure to emphasize his point. "Alright, fine. Please don't hurt him."

The sound of rustling tree limbs caught her attention. She turned to her left. Benjamin surfaced from his hiding place and rejoined the party.

"Benjamin, did you cause the confusion with these two?"

"Yes. It was the first spell that came to mind."

"It looked and sounded very painful. Good work!"

"Thanks."

She glared at the boys as they exchanged pats on the back and smug smiles. Unaware of what else to do, she stood and let them bind her. This time, they bound her arms as well. Secure and back in the wagon, she watched the two boys walk to the big man and the trapped Demarko. Not taking his focus off the man on the ground, the big man pulled another knife from his belt. Holding it at the ready, he instructed his captive to cooperate and let the boys bind him. Demarko stood motionless and obeyed. With his arms tied as tightly as his hands, they loaded him into their rolling prison.

The big man and Bernard grabbed the horses and reattached them to the wagon while Benjamin disappeared back into the woods. He brought back with him the three extra horses they had used to catch up. Upon returning, he used a length of rope and tied the extra horses to the back of the wagon, then took a seat next to his brother up front. With both prisoners apprehended and back in the cart, the three captors once again headed out. Destination unknown.

Chapter Two
Despair and Hope

She sat quietly and watched the trees pass as they rode. The rough terrain only made her already aching muscles scream for release as she continued to be jarred around. Tears dropped from her cheeks, extinguishing the flame of hope. Her future looked doomed and filled with unhappiness. Emotions crowded her mind and swirled like oil in water, making it impossible to sift through. First, confusion and anger, now hopelessness and despair added to the mix. And that was before she could count the feelings wrapped around Demarko and the confusing thoughts surrounding him. The pounding in her head didn't help matters.

Why is this happening? I don't understand any of this. Something isn't right here. They must have me confused with someone else. I have done nothing wrong.

They had traveled for quite a while when Demarko's whispered words broke the silence "Someone must want us alive."

"What gave you that impression? They did just about kill you back there."

"Well, that, I think, was an accident, but that's also part of my point. They had their chance to kill us and didn't. They have fought us only for the purpose of capture. They need us alive wherever we are going."

That made sense. They did seem only eager enough to capture

them. *Maybe I can use this to my advantage.* Focus returned to her mind and a plan had already formed.

"Where are we going?" she asked.

"To see the King."

King? "To see what King?"

As if someone had told a hilarious joke, the laughter from the three up front filled her ears and reddened her face. Blaze turned her attention to Demarko and gave him a puzzling look. He seemed just as lost.

Let's see how far I can run with this. Curiosity, the need for answers, or just plain craziness, she heard herself speak again.

"My mind is a bit fuzzy, but perhaps, if you tell me his name, I will remember." *And be in on the joke.*

Benjamin's eyes locked with hers and he let his disgusted tone fly "Madam, don't play games with me. I'm not stupid enough to believe you don't know your own husband."

Talk about a slap in the face, this was definitely that moment. Pondering it, she faintly remembered she hadn't been alone, but the thought of a husband just evaded her. Air stuck in her lungs as she plummeted into the dark oblivion residing in her head and got lost in her own mind.

King? Husband? Married? Does that mean I'm Queen? How's this possible? Does King mean master? Am I someone's slave? How does Demarko fit in here?

Her head throbbed and she felt as if it might burst through her skull while she tried to work it out. Nausea snaked its way up to her throat and threatened to spill bile on her already dirty dress. She swallowed hard and choked it back. *The last thing I need is to lose what small amount of strength I have left by vomiting.* She looked up and saw Benjamin still glaring at her. He turned to his father and pointed out what seemed clear.

"She truly doesn't remember."

Fools! An errant thought hit her and she decided to test it. "If I'm the Queen, I demand to be treated as such. Untie me at once and explain yourselves! I demand to know who you are."

Her tone, strong and full of authority, surprised her as much as the others. Three faces stared at her for a split second and turned back as if she were nothing of importance. Her blood pressure rose and filled her with the scorching heat of anger. She spiraled dangerously close to panic. *I won't be ignored! I'm just going to have to try a different approach. What do I have to lose? My life? That looks gloomy at best. I have to try!*

She ignored her better judgment and scooted as well as she could toward the front of the wagon, careful to keep her back facing the three imprisoners. She soon found the seat they were sitting on and gently tilted her head to test what sat behind it. She felt one of the boys. *Perfect!* She brought her head forward and slammed it as hard as she could into the soft muscle of the boy's back.

"Ouch!" *Sounds like Benjamin.*

"I asked you a question and I demand an answer now!"

"You want a response, Queen, well here it is."

She scrutinized him as he spoke, his hands moved in patterns in the air above her head. *Now, I know why the sparkle in his eyes is different.* She guessed his intent and feigned passing out.

"Nooo! Did you just kill her?"

"She sleeps, so not another word from you, or you'll sleep, too. I grow tired of these games"

She opened her eyes and looked at Demarko to let him know she had faked it. As soon as she did, she felt slapped yet again, mentally. This time it had been from the hard hand of shame. She felt very close to him. She sensed something there, some kind of connection. Her heart seemed just as jumbled as her mind. If the information is correct, she's a married woman. Linking it all together was more than difficult.

"Do I love this man I am married to? Wouldn't that love keep me from feeling this way about a stranger? Why do I feel something for Demarko if he is not my husband? Exactly what is it I feel for Demarko? Something is wrong, very wrong!

Despair set in as the situation seemed to get worse by the minute. Additional knowledge meant added confusion. The more she tried to work it out, the more her mind just ached. Blaze hated it, but she knew what she had to do. She would just have to wing it. That was never a good plan.

Absorbed in her thoughts, she hadn't noticed the faint orange glow off in the distance, or the numbness in her arms until the sound of Bernard's voice followed by Demarko's brought her back from the brink of darkness.

"Finally, we're close. Shall I wake them?"

"No need. We were never asleep."

Her body swayed back and forth while the wagon milled forward. As they got closer, her vision beheld the path to her demise in the form of a huge castle. The road was visible by two rows of brightly lit torches. The light bounced off the castle walls, causing the shadows to dance. Blaze stared at the enormous enclosure, trying to remember it. Rummaging her brain, she looked for anything solid to link her to this, but nothing came. No matter how hard she tried, not one spark of recognition. She felt out of place to say the least. It was beautiful. It resembled what she would imagine any castle to be. Big, beautiful, heavily guarded, and cold.

"Halt!"

She spied the two guards standing watch at the gate. They were dressed in silver armor that shone radiantly against the light of the flickering flames. They were tall, blonde-haired, and largely built. They definitely looked the part. Their young faces didn't give the impression of inexperience or immaturity. Rather, it helped to enhance the fierce look written across those fine features. Even though they hadn't said much at all, their demeanor spoke volumes. They were deadly serious.

"Time to get out"

Working her way to the back of the wagon, she watched as the two brothers helped Demarko out. The big man, stink and all, walked around and reached up to help her.

"Easy now. I wouldn't want the King to think we were mistreating his Queen."

Fear and alertness had her searching for an exit and an escape plan. Fleeing, she knew, was just a wild hope, but she gave into it anyway. Her gut feeling urged her to stay until the ropes were off and then make a run for it. For now, she had to endure the disgusting captors.

Grubby hands held her tightly and helped her out of the wagon. Her dirty feet stumbled a bit when she put weight on her already shaky legs. His foul breath turned her stomach once more as he leaned in to steady her. Stomach muscles clenched and jaw locked, she fought back the urge to vomit. The closer he got the harder it had been to control. *That chuckling and smile of his is just as nasty as the rest of him.* She forced herself to hold her own and walked to stand beside Demarko. She watched as the leader strode in front of everyone and addressed the guards.

"We're here to see King Deverox. We have found the Queen and one other."

They could only see her face, she figured, due to the fact she stood at the back of the pack. The tallest guard stared at her a long time, and finally went to his knees.

"Welcome home, My Queen."

Soon, everyone else joined him on their knees, bowing before her. It felt odd, yet at the same time, almost familiar. She made herself stand tall as she played along, so she could have a reason to lock her legs that threatened to buckle at any moment. A few moments passed and they all straightened to full height.

The big man was the first to break the silence with his annoying voice and arrogant attitude. "Well, now that all the formalities are over, can we get to the King? I have places to be."

The guards gave him a hard look as if they were going to say something else, but decided on, "Yes we need to get the Queen into her quarters before she catches her death out here."

She followed as the guards marched the party through the large door and into the castle. Once inside, they were led to the entrance hall. Three steps to the right, she moved around the parade to see the room more clearly and hoped the surroundings might ignite the emptiness that had replaced her memories.

The Entrance Hall was warm, but a bit drafty. Along the sides of each wall were rows of chairs. A long table placed at the far end showed a man looking over stacks of parchment. He was an older man, as evident from his graying hair. His shoulders were broad and slightly hunched from his tall workload. He glanced up as the party entered the room. As soon as his eyes locked with hers, he gave the warmest smile. That smile held thankfulness and joy. He stood as the guards approached the table. She eyed everyone and mentally took notes.

"Kip, Kam, thank heavens! You have found the Queen."

Before anyone could say anything, the big man blurted out, "No! I have found the Queen, thank you. My boys and I. This is Benjamin and Bernard." Using his hands, he pointed them out.

The old man rounded on him. "I'm Connery Shaunt, The Magistrate, and who might you be, Mr. Rude?"

"My apologies, Mr. Shaunt. My name is Marcus Harenton. My sons and I found the Queen wondering in the woods with this stranger." Pointing at Demarko, he continued, "As soon as we recognized the Queen, we brought her back here."

Anger filled her from head to toe. She didn't know what her fate would be, but she wouldn't go down alone.

"Why didn't you tell me who you were when you found me unconscious and scared to death? All you volunteered was that I was going on a trip with you and the boys were to tie me up and put me in the wagon. What did you do to me? My mind is blank and fuzzy. All my memories are gone. I can't remember a thing."

Harenton soon began to back track as three angry faces glared at him.

"Kip, check the Queen. Make sure she wasn't mistreated in any way," Shaunt commanded

Gentle hands from the guard inspected her. "Why is she bound like some common criminal? Her clothes are covered in dirt, her hair's in disarray, and her face is streaked with tears."

A bit better, she unwound some. She yelled a little, but most importantly, the ropes were off. With her feet, she pushed them away as soon as they hit the floor. Her fear also seemed to ebb away. The guards and the old man seemed genuine. She still had no idea if any of this was true, but perhaps she wouldn't have to fight for her life. Happy thoughts filled her mind. *Maybe I wasn't delivered into the hands of the enemy after all.* Her body began to relax just a little at the thought of being safe. Jumping a few feet in the air and clutching her hands to her chest, she heard the guard named Kam yell at Mr. Harenton.

"You had better have a real good reason as to why she wasn't treated with the respect befit of a Queen!"

"Please, we meant no disrespect. When we found her, she put up quite a fight and was unaware of who she was. She didn't believe we were there to help her. I assure you, Sir, we had no other choice but to tackle her and knock her out with a sleeping drug. Since she wouldn't cooperate, we soaked the cloth and held it over her nose and mouth until she went limp. The man over there was with her. We knocked him on the back of the head and he went down. We didn't know who he was or why he was in her company. We tied them up so they wouldn't get away because it was dark. They put up quite a fight."

She watched as the guards rounded on Demarko, followed by a tirade of questions. "Who are you? Why were you with the Queen? What were your intentions and what business do you have that constitutes being caught with her without proper verification?"

She had heard enough. "Why are you yelling at him? I'm not sure why he's here, but I can assure you, he treated me better than this terrorizing threesome. He was very kind. They never once said that they were there to help. These three were rude and uncaring. Benjamin used two different spells. One caused us to go blind and the other one put me to sleep when I demanded answers. What were we supposed to think? Of course we defended ourselves."

Her chest heaved and her adrenaline seemed to race her heart. She inhaled deeply and tried to even out her breathing as Kam turned to Demarko to confirm her story.

"Is this true?"

"Yes, it is. My name is Anastas Demarko, but I would prefer Demarko. I admit, I didn't know who she was until Boar and Ass here pointed it out. She was very upset, and with good reason. I was just trying to help. With both our memories gone... We just didn't know."

Demarko looks so defeated, but the guard seems to believe him. Maybe he is done yell...no, I was wrong. More yelling.

"Which one of you is Benjamin and why would you use magic on the Queen? You know it's forbidden."

"I do apologize, but they were being very...difficult to handle, Sir."

"What spell did you use and does it have a counter spell that needs to be done?" Mr. Shaunt asked.

"I'm new, still learning...I...I used Enemy Dilation. It doesn't need a counter. It stopped when my concentration was broken."

"What does it do? What was its purpose?" Kip Demanded

"As I said, they are fine with no permanent damage," he defended. Seeing three unsatisfied faces still glaring in his direction, he continued, "The spell causes the eye pupils to dilate. When the pupils dilate, they let in more light. The spell caused their pupils to open almost completely, rendering them unable to see..." Before he could answer any further, Kam had struck him hard against the face.

At that very moment, she knew she had been right about one thing. They indeed were deadly serious. She felt proud and worried at the same time. *I hope they are truly on my side and that I won't ever have to tangle with them. If what they say is true, perhaps they have to do what I say. They said I'm their Queen. Then again, there is the matter of who really rules this place. King Deverox, it seems. I might not be a safe as I thought.*

The guard didn't shy away after striking the young man. He simply followed the boy's body to the ground and continued to scorn him. She almost felt sorry for him...almost!

"Are you completely ignorant? That could have caused major damage, you fool. The Queen could have gone blind for real. Magic is not a game. Thank the heavens that your concentration was broken."

Soon, the guard stood in front of her waving his hand in front of her face. "How many fingers do you see, My Queen?"

"Thr—"

She heard a commotion to her right and noticed the boy as he got off the floor. When he stood, he looked once to his father and then back at the guards. "I assure you, she's fine. I swear. I had no other choice…"

How can he move so fast in all that heavy armor?

"Oh, you had a choice, young man. She's the Queen of Pedalstem and as such, is as delicate as a flower. You can't convince me, boy, that you had no choice. Where Demarko is concerned, you can't expect a man not to defend himself."

The boy glanced at everyone in the room with a look of disgust on his face and pushed his luck further. "Delicate as a flower? Don't let her size fool you. She's fury trapped in a cracked bottle. There's more to her than a pretty face. She put all she had into fighting us off and yet for some reason she was…I'm not sure if *holding back* is the right description…she seemed to be giving it all, but…trust me there's more to her—no, to both of them. There's more to both of them," Benjamin explained.

Hand half in the air, she almost asked the boy what he meant when Mr. Shaunt spoke and cut her off.

"Guards, untie this Demarko fellow." He turned toward the undesirables and added, "As for you three, have a seat over there and I'll see what should be done with you."

Blaze laid her hand in his gentle grasp when he reached for her and softly said, "Come, My Queen. I will take you inside. Demarko, I'm certain the King would like a word with you also. Boys, make sure our guests stay here until I return."

She glanced back at the guards and saw that they had the three men sitting in chairs. The unwanted guests each wore looks of fear. The guards were trading glances, with smirks spread across their faces. They truly liked guard duty. She really hoped she never had to cross either of them.

As she entered the throne room, it left her breathless. It was large, beautiful, and elaborately decorated. Long banquet tables lined each side, each with white Lilies as a centerpiece. Down the center of the floor ran a red carpet with intricately embroidered lilies in the middle. It led up to a granite platform and held two enormous thrones. The King's throne was made of pure gold embellished with silver and Diamond scroll patterns. A large Ruby sat atop it. The Queen's throne was identical except instead of a Ruby, it held an Emerald. Just as the lilies were the centerpiece of the tables, the thrones were the focal point for the entire room. Being off balance a bit caused her to fall into Shaunt and prompted his concern.

"Is something wrong, My Queen? Have you become ill? You look as though you might faint."

Inhaling deeply, she whispered, "No, I'm fine."

Fine isn't' the right word. Confused, on edge, and exhausted. Those words describe my feelings better. Not wanting to go into it, she dismissed it all together. She felt vaguely aware of her feet moving her forward. Shaunt led her to her throne and helped her to sit.

"Rest. I shall get the King for you. "

His face turned to Demarko. "Please have a seat over there at one of the tables and make yourself comfortable."

Blaze felt like a small child as Shaunt gave her a once over to be sure he could leave. Her body seemed fine. It was her mind that had gone on sabbatical. Weariness took its hold and she feared she might pass out. Willpower alone kept her eyes from closing. *I need sleep. I need answers. First, I need to get out of here. I don't know if I can really trust these people. They seem sincere, but who knows? I just need to be left alone so that I can figure this out. I feel like a misbehaving teen that has run away.* Air left her lungs and she relaxed when the man moved away from her. As Shaunt headed toward the door, she heard the sound of a second door bursting open as a woman ran in.

"Thank goodness, Shaunt. I heard the Queen was returned. Is she well?"

Before she could register an answer or respond, Shaunt intervened.

"She is fine, Arabella," he responded as he gestured in her direction. "She looks as though she might faint. I think she may need hot tea to help calm her nerves. She has had a difficult time."

The pair left the room with their heads huddled together,

whispering. She chanced a glance at Demarko and noticed he sat patiently at the tables as if he were waiting to be served. A few moments later, her attention turned to Arabella bustling back into the room.

She was a short frumpy woman. Her gray hair was pulled tightly against her scalp with the exception of the stray strands that refused to stay in place. She looked as though she worked very hard. The dress she wore was tinted a light purple color with a white apron over it. The grease, food and water stains suggested it had been a rough day in the kitchen. As quickly as the old woman moved, the folded towel perched over her shoulder stayed in place perfectly. The tray she carried held a small teapot, two cups, and some fresh muffins, Blueberry by the smell of them. The serving dish seemed to float right above her hand.

"Here, dear, have some tea." Arabella turned to Demarko. "Please come here, young man."

She tried not to, but she stared as he strode from the table and headed her direction. The way he walked seemed just as enticing as the rest of him. He exuded confidence, but not to the point of arrogance. With her body temperature through the roof and feeling a blush on her cheeks, she watched his muscles tighten with each movement. *Where Demarko is concerned I hope this is a dream. The rest is a horrifying nightmare.*

If this was a dream, that would explain her immoral attraction to Demarko and most of her memory malfunction. Pinching her left arm, she tested for pain to see if it were real or dreamed. *Ouch! Defiantly real.* Now, the question was, what to do about it. Infatuation with Demarko put a kink in her dreamy reality. Not only could she not forget she was a married woman, she was also a Queen. The complications this would cause if she couldn't get it under control were overwhelming.

As Blaze drank her tea, she tried to block it out for now. Her body ached, her head throbbed, and her muscles cried out for relaxation. All she could do was to relax until she could think of a way out of it. Demarko's voice and presence dropped her head from the clouds and brought her heavily back to her chaotic life.

"Yes, ma'am, what can I do for you?"

"No, no, nothing. Would you like some tea?" Arabella pushed the tea into his hands, gave him a warm smile, and indicated for him to have a seat on the platform.

Chapter Three
Kings and Dreams

Engrossed in conversation and sipping tea, she didn't hear anyone join them. She jumped, her cup almost falling from her hands, when someone's presence and loud voice invaded the room.

"Thank goodness you are alive, Blaze. Where have you been?"

He must be the King. He towered over her as she sat in the throne. Blaze knew she should say or do something. She tried to speak, but the sight of him left her speechless. She didn't know this man. Nothing was recognizable—not his face, his voice, or his demeanor. Her memory was still blank as parchment. Her gut told her she should respond somehow, but her mind seemed too busy doing acrobatic flips to form words. Her only option would be to watch the scene unfold. King Deverox turned to Demarko, anger in his tone.

"Shaunt tells me you were brought in with my wife, and you were with her when they found you. I would like to know why!"

Something he said struck her wrong. *Wife? Didn't he mean to say queen? Why ask the question that way? Perhaps I'm over analyzing this.* Demarko's sad voice broke her heart as he spoke.

"I wish I could say, My Lord, but I simply don't remember. My mind is still very frayed. As for the Queen, I'm not sure I was *with* her. She's unknown to me. As Queen, I assume I should, but I just don't remember anything at all. I'm sorry to disappoint you."

Her heart rate accelerated due to anxiety that set in as she continued to watch. Demarko looked ashamed of something he had no control over. The King's face wore an expression of uncertainty. *He doesn't' believe him. Why would Demarko lie? What could he gain from that? Uh, oh.* The King's face flashed from one version of red to another. *I don't have to remember him to know what that means.* Her intuition sent a red flag that had her worried for Demarko's safety. *He looks as if he might strike Demarko dead where he stands.* Her chest got tight and adrenaline took over. *I have to do something.* She followed her instincts and flew out of the throne to speak to the King.

"My Lord, please, I'm sure he's telling the truth. I, too can't remember anything. I was hoping that you might be able to fill in the blanks for me. I suspect that those men who supposedly found us have done something. When I awoke, my head was buzzing. I remembered nothing. It's as if I was drugged, or something. My mind is still uncooperative."

Jumping up quickly had caused her head to spin and the world to tilt. She swayed on her feet as the dizziness set in yet again. The soft hands of a woman encased her body when her knees gave out and a soft whisper filled her ears. Before she could right herself, she seemed to drop in the chair and her vision filled with the King's face—his breath on her skin and his eyes locked onto hers. She froze. His pupils were strange and different. His expression was full of concern, but the fire that danced in his eyes didn't match the rest of his face. After a moment, he pulled away and stood up. *His eyes are frightening.*

"I think we should get her to bed soon. We can discuss this in the morning. Shaunt, would you show Demarko to one of the guest rooms, please. Demarko, I ask that you stay in your room until we call for you."

Blaze found herself in King Deverox's tight grasp. Her frame held in his embrace, he pulled her upright and forced her onto her feet. Unable to stand on her own, she leaned weakly into him. Her arm around his neck, her feet and toes shuffled quickly across the floor as he practically dragged her through the door behind the throne platform. He moved too quickly, but she tried to take in as much of the hall as possible and map her surroundings.

Long colorful tapestries hung along the stone walls in neat rows. They depicted different garden scenes. King Deverox's face wore that same look of concern when she looked back at him. *Perhaps he's just worried I will pass out and that's why he's in a hurry.* She forced herself to stand, her head a little swimmy, and she felt his hands slide from her waist as he opened the door.

"I will get some bath water ready and warm the bathing room for you. I'm sure you would like to wash some of that dirt off you. You always like to soak in the bath after a stressful day."

Blaze staggered into the room and glanced in every direction. The bedchamber looked pleasing to the eye. She stumbled and fell onto the bed. The room itself seemed as big as the comfortable bed she sat on. She noticed the large soft pillows matched its coverlet. The linen was all white and fashioned with lilies embroidered on the fabric in gold stitching. A blazing fire roared in the fireplace. It helped to warm the area from the center wall. To the left stood an enormous bookshelf overflowing with books that sat nicely next to a well-used divan. Between the light from the fireplace and the gold sconces on the wall, the room had a nice glow to it.

I must enjoy reading. As her eyes swept over the shelf she noted the extensive volumes shoved neatly into place. *Perhaps one of these books will help me figure out what's going on and maybe who I am.* Her bearings seemed back on track. She pushed off the soft mattress and walked over to investigate the titles. Her hand on the spine of a book, she jumped when his voice sounded behind her.

"Nice and toasty, your water is ready, my dear. I have hung your favorite robe next to the tub for you."

His arm wrapped around her shoulders, he led her into the bathing room. The aroma of lavender and vanilla filled her senses and her body and mind began to soften and relax. Her eyes wandered down to the tub and what she saw surprised her. Fresh lavender flowers floated along the surface, turning the water a soft purple color.

Butterflies swarmed in her stomach. Not sure what to say, she decided to press her luck. She faced him and noticed something. For some reason, it struck her as odd. She found looking at him seemed quite different from gazing upon Demarko. The two were at opposite ends of the spectrum.

His frame was long and lean, but not muscular, and stood a few inches taller. His dark slick hair started at the top of his head and drove straight down until it stopped just short of his shoulders. His outfit was unique. A long-sleeved black satin shirt pressed and fit well against his frame. Ruby buttons ran up the side and added a certain kind of flair. The oddest part about it was the sinister red eyes stitched into the fabric right over his heart. His black pants hugged his midsection and legs all the way down to his knees and tucked neatly into dark leather boots. He fashioned a large Ruby around his neck attached to a woven leather neckband.

I can see how other women may find him attractive. Well, maybe. His pearly smooth skin stretched over his square jaw and fine facial features, but when you got to the eyes... *His eyes held you in place with the shear fear of them.* They were round amber stones encased in red-rimmed fire. Blaze tried to look away, but found she couldn't. *Scary and captivating.* The race was now on between her heart and pulse to see which would be faster. *I'm going to have to walk softly around this man. He's dangerous. His face and his soft touch seem to say I can trust him, but those eyes just scream mayhem. I'm not sure where I rank here...ally or enemy? Time will tell soon enough. He is either sincere or he's not, his actions will put truth his words.*

Cool hands and fingers brushed her skin when he tried to pull off her dress. Her hands flew up and she grabbed his wrists in protest and hoped he wouldn't go any further.

"I think I can handle it from here, thank you. If it's okay, I would prefer some alone time to relax and unwind."

Holding her breath, she waited for his reaction. *Good or bad, I have to follow through.*

"As you wish, my love. I understand. I have a few matters to attend to anyway. I'll return in a while to check on you. I'm grateful that you are home safe. I love you."

She stared into his face for a moment and saw a look of expectancy as if he were awaiting a response. She couldn't bring herself to say those three little words she knew he wanted to hear. *What do I do? What is the right thing to say? I love you? That doesn't feel right. I feel as though I don't even know him. How can I say I love you to someone I don't remember?* Her focus went back to his face and she saw a small smile there, almost reaching his eyes. Seeming to catch her thoughts, she assumed, he kissed her hand and left the room. She felt faint once again, only this time she felt as if she had evaded the hangman's noose. *Whew. I thought for sure that would get ugly. I'm not sure what is going on, but his touch feels odd to me. None of this makes sense. It just seems twisted and strange.* Quietly, she stood listening, and waited for his footsteps to disappear, then pulled the dress off her shoulders and let it drop to the floor.

She stepped into the bath and it was heavenly. The water, inviting and warm, felt delightful against her skin. It instantly soothed her. She found it hard not to relax with the warmth from the bath and the calming aroma from the flowers. Finally, she gave in, lay back, and closed her eyes. Submerged in water, her body felt warm and her mind seemed to slow. Her aching muscles rejoiced and the throb in her head dissipated.

A few moments later, she opened her eyes and scanned the small room. It wasn't as elaborate as the rest, but still held much beauty. Behind her, a large pedestal held a crystal vase filled with an extravagant arrangement of flowers, Lilies, Aster, and Wisteria. Next to the large deep tub, sitting in the center, stood a tall golden rod that held her robe. Off in the far corner, half hidden by a partition, sat her chamber pot. It looked clean and new. She noticed the outside of the tub crafted of green marble, fashioned veins of gold running through it. This room was definitely beautiful, but paled in comparison to what she had seen so far.

Even with her body relaxed, weariness urged her to get out and lie down. She reached for her robe and heard someone enter her bedchamber. She froze halfway out of the tub, straining her ears in an attempt to find out who had entered. She heard the sound of light movements. *Well, I'm positive I don't want to be caught unaware and naked, so I think I'll skip drying off and just slip on the robe.* Silk stuck to her wet skin, as she quietly crept over to the door and peeked around the wooden frame. A sigh of relief washed over her when she saw the old woman who had brought her hot tea. As she strode in from the bathing room, the woman turned to her.

"I'm sorry to have disturbed you. I was just bringing more tea and stoking the fire for you."

"Thank you. I was getting out when you came in so you didn't disturb me. I'm sorry, but I really can't remember who you are."

"Don't be sorry, dear. I'm Arabella Collingsworth, the head maid and cook around here. I understand that your mind is giving you trouble, but I'm sure in no time, we will be friends once more. Would you like some tea before bed?"

She has a sweet demeanor. She looks trustworthy. "That would be nice thank you. So, we're friends then?"

"Of course, dear. We can talk more tomorrow. How about you just rest for now?"

Feet on the cool floor, she crossed the room, pulled back the covers, and crawled into bed. The chill of the linen plus the wet robe plastered to her skin caused her body to tremble slightly. *Yes, hot tea was very nice.* Both hands wrapped around the cup, she felt the warmth radiating through her fingers, winding its way up her arms. Unaware of what to say, she watched the woman bustle around. When she finished, Arabella left and shut the door, leaving her to sip her tea alone.

Today has been brutal. Exhaustion and fatigue threatened to shut her down, but her mind wound up once again and worked overtime. Even though she felt a little more relaxed, fear and confusion still had a tight grasp. Confused because she didn't know what happened, afraid if she went to sleep, she would awaken to find herself somewhere else and this day would start all over again.

Looking around the room didn't help to bring back any memories. That was heart breaking. Tears rolled down her cheeks due to pure frustration and distress. Reason and understanding were staying hidden from her. Alone and frightened, she felt as if she had indeed lost her mind.

Cold wet hair stuck to her thin robe. A draft in the room blew across her, causing chills to dance upon her skin. She put the tea on the table and snuggled under her soft blankets. She closed her eyes and a few breaths later, a young red haired woman filled her dreams…

"I still like him a lot, Arabella. I mean I look at him and I get a funny feeling in my stomach, and suddenly, I don't know what to say. My mouth won't move, but my mind is off on a tangent filled with questions. Does he like me? Does he think I'm pretty? I just don't understand what's going on…Why are you laughing?"

"Here, have some tea before your hysteria completely takes over and I have to dunk you in the water barrel. I'll talk you through this."

Sipping her tea, she nodded and tried to calm down. "Thank you."

"You're welcome, Red. Let me guess…when you look at him, you like what you see?

"Yes, he's fetching."

Eyes staring dizzyingly at the ceiling, his face entered her mind. Her heart pounded, her pulse raced, and her head suddenly felt lighter than air. Two clicks in her ear from the snapping of fingers brought her back to the present.

"Oh, I'm sorry. I will try and focus, but sometimes it's hard."

"That's okay. I bet you want to sit close to him, maybe hold his hand?"

"Yes—I mean no…okay, yea."

"Red, you are growing into a fine young woman. I imagine that Woody thinks so, too. You are sixteen now and you view things differently, especially boys. It's perfectly natural. Before, it was, I wonder if he wants to go outside and play. Now, I wonder if he wants to be my boyfriend."

Hands folded around the small cup, mouth full of tea, and she choked when that word filled the kitchen.

"Shhh! Boyfriend? You know Father will kill us both. He can't be my boyfriend. I'm not sure I want him to be…my…boyfriend."

Her body still, hands frozen in place, she thought about what Arabella had said and something clicked.

"Thank you. I love you so much. I do want him to ask me to be his girlfriend. He's handsome and charming. Hey, where are the twins today? I almost didn't come in here and talk to you because I thought they might be here."

"I'm sure they are around here somewhere."

"At least I didn't have to talk about some other girl problem. That was embarrassing, but this seemed more private."

"What's private?" Kipper asked.

"Right on cue," Arabella said quietly.

"You know we can keep a secret, Red. We would only tell each other. And look, we are both here so we wouldn't be lying when we say we won't repeat it," Kamron said.

"No way am I telling you two clowns. This is something between your mother and me."

Smiling at the twins and enjoying the banter, she tried to keep from laughing at them. Kipper placed his hand over his heart and put a faked hurt expression on his face.

"That hurts, Red, hurts deep," Kipper said.

"Yeah, real deep. You think we can't be trusted," Kamron replied.

One hand on her stomach, the other over her mouth, and unable to contain it, she laughed. "Whatever. You are not the least bit hurt."

"Yeah, you're right. Oh, well, guess we will have to torture it out of you," Kamron stated.

The sound of the twins chanting in tune bounced off the walls. "Red's got a secret…Red's got a secret…" they sang.

She watched the boys skipping out of the room, laughing the whole way and didn't notice someone else enter from the back door.

"What are those two going on about now?" Woody asked.

She froze and her breathing stopped when she heard his voice. Pulling herself together and gathering her thoughts, she turned and answered Woody.

"You know those two will do anything to get a rise out of someone."

"That sounds like them, alright. Um, Red, can I talk to you please...outside?" he asked.

"Sure."

Glancing at Arabella and getting nothing but a shrug and a broad smile, she followed him out the door. Coming to halt, she looked up and was face to face with Woody. So close, too close. Those eyes... *His breath on her cheeks and her head suddenly in his hands, she closed her eyes and found herself kissing him back. Red stood on her toes and electricity ran laps up her spine. His hands encircled her waist and she almost fainted. Catching her breath, she looked at him when he stepped away. Blush on her cheeks and heat in her face, she hoped he didn't mistake her happiness for embarrassment.*

"I'm sorry. That's not what I called you out here for. You were just so close...I wanted...I mean what I asked you out here for is to see if you wanted to go with me to the Fall Festival tomorrow?"

Taking two steps, closing the distance between them, she wrapped her arms around his neck and kissed him again... Electrifying. I can feel everything—the grass thorough my shoes, the sun through my clothes, and his emotions in his touch. Magical!

"Ahem."

Stopping abruptly, she dropped her arms, turned around, and tried licking the evidence from her lips. Holding her hands behind her back and wearing an innocent expression, she faced Arabella and awaited her fate.

"That'll be quite enough, you two. Time to come up for air. I need help with this candy."

"We'll be right there...promise."

She felt his arm around her waist and his side against her back. She looked at him and giggled. "I thought we were caught for sure."

"I did, too. So, is it safe to assume we'll be going to the festival together?"

Placing her arm around his waist and leaning into him, she answered, "Yes."

Chapter Four
The New Beginning

Getting off the platform and intent on walking to the tables, Demarko stopped when he heard Shaunt yell his name. Twisting his frame, he faced the man. "Yes, Mr. Shaunt?"

"Demarko, King Deverox has asked that I make preparations for you this evening. I'm here to show you to the guest rooms. If you'll come with me, please."

He followed the magistrate through the entrance hall and to a door on the left side of the room. As he stepped through, his eyes found that the long hall held large tapestries along the walls. Some held glorious pictures of the King and Queen and some featured small villages. *The Queen looks as if she fits in that picture, but…the King…hmm I don't know.* Under each wall hanging, a perfectly centered table sat adorned with small trinkets and vases full of flowers. The draft from the windows danced along his skin and caused the flames in the sconces to sway back and forth.

Tight muscles, cramping legs, and a weary body ached for the prospect of comfort. His mind was a blur and his limbs reacted on forced commands. Mentally, he blocked out the pain and fatigue as he continued to trail the old man. Suddenly, he stopped. He noticed Mr. Shaunt had keys in the lock of the wooden door. *Tink, tink tink,* echoed down the hall as the keys banged together at the twisting and turning movements. Shaunt opened the door and stood aside, urging him in as he spoke.

"This'll be your room for the night. The King has left instructions that you stay until he has spoken with you."

He stepped into the room and watched as Shaunt quickly pointed out the bed and the direction to the chamber pot. He smiled once and left. Demarko checked his accommodations, noting it to be huge and elaborate. *That bed looks very inviting—big and soft.* He forced his legs to carry him over and sit on the edge of the mattress. Reaching down, he slipped out of his boots. *That feels nice.* He wiggled his toes to relieve some of the cramping.

Demarko scooted toward the headboard, laid his head on the soft pillow and waited for sleep to overtake him. *Oh, of course.* Sliding from the bed, he went in search of the chamber pot. Up and around, he noticed a writing desk to his left and a small bookshelf to his right. His bladder threatening to let go at any moment, he hurried past both pieces of furniture and walked through the door to the bathing room.

Both rooms had a soft glow illuminated by sconces on the wall. He shuffled his feet quickly over to the corner. Head back, one hand on the wall and eyes closed, he let the relief wash over him. Feeling better, he turned to go back, but something he missed caught him by surprise.

In his haste, he had overlooked the bathtub. Steam twirled into the air from the water. He dropped down and tested the temperature. *Huh, this must've been drawn right before I arrived.* Bottom of his shirt in hand, he peeled it off his chest. Hand on the top of his pants, he prepared to drop them, too, but heard a woman's voice from the outer room.

"Mr. Demarko? It's Arabella. I've come to collect your dirty clothes and give you some clean ones. May I come in?"

He picked up his shirt and walked out to speak with the maid. "You may come in. I'm covered."

A little confused, he looked from her outstretched hand back to her face and she spoke.

"Here's some night garments," she said, placing them across the bed. "I'll need those dirty clothes, young man. I'll have them cleaned and ready for you by sunrise."

I can't just strip them off in front of her. Oh, I know. He handed her his shirt and smiled. "Okay…give me just a minute."

Once in the chamber room, he pulled off his pants and wrapped a small towel around his waist for cover. *That's better.* Now, less exposed, he walked back into the room where she waited with her hand still out. The concrete under his feet felt cool as he walked the remaining distance to the woman. His pants now in her possession, she smiled at him as she turned to leave. He glanced at the outfit and noticed a long men's sleeping gown. *That looks like a dress, light blue satin and ruffles. No way am I wearing that.*

"Sunrise, I promise."

He reached out and gently grabbed her arm. "Wait, Ms. Arabella."

"Yes, dear?"

"Is Blaze—I mean, how is the Queen? She was pretty unstable. Is she all right?"

"Yes. She is fine. I just left her room and she was sipping hot tea and heading for bed. There is no need to worry, dear. Your Queen's in safe hands, and speaking of rest, I do believe that you need some. Would you like me to bring you some hot tea?"

"No. Thank you, anyway."

"Well, if you require anything, the maid's quarters are located at the end of the hall."

He watched as she left the room, closing the door behind her. Body still, eyes locked on the closed door, his thoughts wandered to her again. *So beautiful and brave.* Blaze filled his mind. Her soft skin, her brilliant smile, and of course her vibrant green eyes. He traveled the length of her shapely figure from her bright red spirals to her soft small feet. His body trembled slightly as he remembered the electricity and heat the slightest touch brought on. Heart pounding faster in his chest, his pulse picked up and his whole body smiled at the simple thought of his love for her. *Why is my love for her so deep? Is it because she's Queen? It can't be. Perhaps it's not love, but admiration and fascination.* He shook his head, refocused his eyes, and tried to dislodge the lust from his mind. He knew thinking of her in that way was wrong. However, he was having a hard time breaking free of it.

As he forced his worn out legs to carry him back to the bathing room, he dropped his towel and stepped into the tub. Soap in hand, he moved it vigorously as he washed the dirt and grime away. Fresh water and the smell of soap filled his nose and sent a relaxing feeling through him. With his eyes closed, he basked in the peace and tranquility of the moment. Mind and muscles relaxed helped to clear his head a little. Soon, his body craved the softness of the bed and the stillness of sleep. Demarko leaned forward, filled his palms with water, and splashed it on top of his head scrubbing his scalp.

Clean and smelling better, he stood, grabbed the small fluffy fabric and stepped out of the tub. Water dripped from his skin and collected into a small pool at his feet. Towel in hand, he moved the cotton cloth to dry himself. When he looked up, he spotted a small mirror next to the washbasin. As he stared at his reflection, it showed he had acquired new cuts and bruises during his flight for freedom. *That's odd.* He examined the top of his chest closer and found discoloration in the shape of a circle around his neck. *Am I missing a neckband or something?* Balling up his fists, he tried to fight back the frustration. *Not knowing anything about anything is overwhelming. No matter how hard I try, nothing works—just empty space and a black void. I can't even remember the simplest things. Is this to be my fate...never knowing what or who I am? Just me, in this moment, from now on.* Eyes closed, teeth clenched together, he breathed deeply and attempted to calm down. He gripped the sink on both sides and held on for dear life. Finally, he exhaled and calmed his nerves in order to focus.

Towel around his waist, he walked back to the front room, intent on sleep. When he placed one knee on the bed, he heard a loud knocking on the door echoing off the walls. He pushed off and walked to the door. Once open, the two guards, Kip and Kam, stood staring at him. Mouths open, ready to speak, their voices stopped him before a word could pass his lips.

"King Deverox's here to see you, Mr. Demarko."

His stomach muscles clenched tightly, followed by a strong

feeling of *something's just not right.* Each name independently brought no signs of warning, but put the two together…seemed the equivalent of calling a woman, mister. *King Deverox.* It just didn't fit. It sounded wrong. The King's voice began to bring him back to the here and now. *Why do I feel like I hate him? Do I know him to be a bad person?*

He stepped aside as if he had a choice in the matter. "Come in."

"How are your accommodations?"

He watched the King look around the room as if checking the area. "Fine, My Lord. Thank you for your generosity."

He took a step back as King Deverox looked at him with suspicious eyes before starting his monologue.

"I don't know you, or anything about you. That leads me to believe you are foreign to my kingdom. Therefore, I'm unsure if I can trust you. I would like to know what your plans are. There are many kingdoms and the next isn't far away."

"I assure you, My Lord, I'm trustworthy. I haven't any plans of conspiracy against the crown. Let's be honest. Even if that were the case, with my memory gone, I would have no ideas as to my previous plans."

"Since you have no memory of who you are and, obviously no gold, I make this offer to you, and I will only offer it once. You may stay here with no gold, no memory, and no way to provide for yourself. I have only given my word of your welfare for the night, and no more. On the other hand, I can give you enough gold that you would never have to worry about whether or not you were good at a specific trade. You could start anew and make it up as you go along. I would personally escort you in my carriage, which has plenty of food, and drink for the journey. As I say, it is up to you and I only offer this now. Should you decline it… Think about it, Demarko, no gold makes it hard to survive, and with no memory…well, you would have a hard path to follow. "

"You are too kind, but I can't allow you to hand me gold I didn't earn. It's not right. I understand it will be hard, but I must decline the offer."

King Deverox continued to glare at him, his lips pressed in a hard line. He wasn't sure about the King's intentions, but they didn't feel sincere. Emotionless words, nothing more. He spoke again with a tone of superiority

"What are you to do, then?"

"If it pleases, My Lord, with your permission, in the morning, I will venture out into the town to see about work and maybe take up residence at the Inn Dever."

What's with the evil smirk? It screams mayhem! Ding, ding, ding. That was just the signal he had been waiting for. *I can't shake the feeling. I know him and he's up to no good. I'm not going anywhere. Something is off and I aim to find out. Blaze could be in trouble.* Planting his feet firmly on the ground and standing tall, he awaited the King's response.

"Your life…or *death*."

He noted that the King put a heavy emphasis on the death part. King Deverox forced what looked like might be a smile and left the room, guards trailing behind. His instincts took over and told him he needed to be very careful around the King. His impression of the man seemed comparable to thin ice with a large crack. *Very dangerous!*

His body feeling drained, he decided to go and lie down to get some rest. Stretched out and comfortable, his thoughts began in earnest again. He just couldn't figure out what went wrong and why his memory took what seemed to be a permanent vacation. His eyes finally closed and he soon fell asleep.

Muscles relaxed and body unwound, he was very thankful for his restful sleep. His eyes turned up to the ceiling, he thought about what had happened and what he might do about it. A soft knock at the door pulled him from his mind. *I'm quite popular around here.* He threw the covers off and got out of bed.

The cool air flowed over him and chills shook his body, slightly. The feel of fabric that rubbed his skin as it fell, reminded him to look for his clothes. Good to her word, his clean garments were laid over the two chests at the end of the bed. He quickly pulled on his pants and yelled toward the door.

"Just a moment."

Nakedness covered, he reached out and opened the door. A short, tiny-framed woman stood staring up at him with big brown eyes. The steady rocking on her heels left her soft, short curls bouncing around her ears. She wore the oddest expression across her face. She, just as everyone else, seemed unfamiliar to him. Demarko waited only a few seconds for her to respond, but when she only stared, he spoke, instead.

"Can I help you?"

"Oh, Arabella sent me to check on you. I didn't mean to wake you. I did try to knock quietly. My instructions were to just knock, look in, and see that you were well. Please forgive me."

"It's fine. No, harm done." Smiling down at her, he added, "What's your name?"

"Maize."

"Nice to meet you, Maize. I'm Demarko." He nodded. "You can go back and tell her I'm quite well."

As he went to turn away and finish getting dressed, he noticed the woman still standing in the doorway. He turned back and asked, "Is there something else?"

"Do I know you? You look very familiar."

"I don't know. *Do* you know me? Body frozen in place, heart pounding and palms sweating, he anticipated what she would say. Demarko listened intently. *Does she know something? Will I find out who I am?*

"No...maybe you just look like someone I know."

Dammit! Body and hope deflated, he turned back to the room and walked to his clothes so he could finish dressing. Arms in his sleeves, he heard the woman's sweet little voice again as he tugged his shirt into place.

"May I ask you a question?"

He sat on the bed, pulled his boots close, and started to put them on as he answered her. "Yes, you may."

The question turned into a tirade of questions.

"What are you going to do now? Why were you found with the Queen? Do you know the Queen? Where were you two going?

What happened?"

Boots on and ready to go, he walked out of the room and several more people joined in who shouted even more questions.

When will this end? It's not as if I have any answers. His head hurt. He felt as if someone had plucked him from his life and dropped it into another world. Nothing made sense. No one had answers…just endless questions. He forced himself to be calm. He kept the smile on his face and pleasantness in his tone as he answered those questions with same answer.

"I don't know."

After all, they just wanted answers, too. This place was a vortex of confusion. As he reached the door, it held quite a surprise. His hand on the door at the end of the hall had quieted the inquisitors. He decided to test that theory. He dropped his hands and just as he expected, the questions filled his ears again. His hands on the handle…complete silence. Curiosity took over. He turned and asked a question of his own.

"Why is it when I'm about to open the door, all of you stopped asking questions?"

Maize stepped forward. "We don't know if King Deverox's behind that door. We don't want…" She looked around as if she were making sure the coast was clear. "To get in his way."

Don't want to get in his way? He let it go. He felt there was more to it. The fear in their faces showed there *was* more to it. *There's something going on here. I hope he's not mean and cruel to these people.* Turning back to the door, he pulled it open and entered the entrance hall.

* * * *

A hand banged loudly on the door and woke Blaze. She sat straight up in bed and grasped her blankets tightly. Breathing heavy from the sudden noise, she looked around, checking her surroundings. The knocking began again, followed by King Deverox's loud voice.

"Blaze? Are you awake? May I come in?" He asked in a loud

tone that sounded angry.

She rubbed the sleep from her eyes. "Yes, you may enter." *Why is he angry and yelling?*

"You will have to unlock the door. Why did you lock it in the first place?

Locked? I don't remember locking the door.

Feet on the floor, she felt the chill of the cold air bite at her skin as she raced to open the door. Her feet stumbled over one another when he pushed her aside and charged into the room. She grabbed the frame of the door tightly to regain her balance. Steady now, she walked back toward the bed and waited. His face and voice had changed from anger to concern in the length of a heartbeat. She noticed him turn and look at her.

"Are you all right? Why did you lock the door? I thought someone had gotten in here…"

She watched him advance on her. When he got close, he dropped his head and his voice.

"I'm sorry that I have awakened you, but I intended to peek in and found the door locked. I got worried. I'm truly sorry."

She tried to focus the haze of sleep away as she stammered, "It's fine, I guess. I didn't realize that I locked the door. I must have. I was so tired after Arabella left." A moment later, his arms wrapped around her frame and his voice flowed softly in her ear.

"Well, I'm glad you are safe. Here, let me help you back to bed so you may rest."

She allowed him to do just that and covered her legs with the blankets as she sat with her back against the wall. The haze had cleared and she remembered yesterday. It was a blessing and a curse. She knew her surroundings, but had no idea of what happened. Still held in the grip of confusion, she refused to sleep more. Her muscles were relaxed, the throbbing in her head gone, and her stomach growled.

"No, no that's fine. I'm awake now. Actually, My Lord, I'm very hungry. I think I would like something to eat."

"That is marvelous."

Blaze folded her legs under her frame as he sat on the bed and reached for her. She tilted her head slightly upward in order to breathe around his tight embrace. When he pulled away, she looked into his face.

"You are the Queen, yes, but also my wife, so you don't have to call me, *My Lord.* You may call me by my name—Slaine."

She focused on his face, pondering that name and hoping it might spark something. *Slaine. King Deverox. My husband, Slaine. This is of no help. None of it fits. More pieces to the puzzle that has become my life.* The sound of him clearing his throat urged her to acknowledge his reply.

"Oh, sure. I guess, I just forgot. My mind is still blank."

She felt a blush rise on her cheeks. His response surprised her. He stepped to the side of the bed and held his arm out. She got up and headed toward the door. He had her arm in a tight grip. Instinctively, she swung her body around. Her eyes moved from his hand on her arm to his face. She glared at him. *I hate being manhandled.* Never taking her eyes from his, she waited to see what the next second had in store. Blaze knew this was dangerous, but she still didn't back down. *If he had a problem, he could've asked.* The next heartbeat came and went, then he smiled and his voice filled the air as he let go.

"Would you like to change first, or have you decided that your dressing gown is now proper attire for feasting?"

That was an overreaction. Keeping me from embarrassing myself seemed to be his intention. She rubbed her arm and felt her face heat up again. Her head dropped and she closed her eyes, trying to calm down. Softly, she whispered, "Yes, I suppose. I was so hungry, I hadn't realized the lack of clothing. Sorry."

His hand below her chin, he pushed it up forcing her to look at him. His eyes had softened and so did his tone

"That's all right. Don't be so hard on yourself. It'll take some time to get well."

His face sported a smile, and soon, she felt her body pressed against his when he hugged her. Trapped in his embrace for a long moment, she decided it felt strange and foreign, but not dangerous. *I need to accept the way things are and stop fighting them. I still have no memories, but I haven't been delivered into the lion's den. I don't recognize anything about him, but he is my husband. I should at least try. He loves me, obviously, and I'm making this a fight for survival. He hasn't tried to do anything but care for me. I'm a terrible person.* Released from his hold, she tried to hide the tears upon her face.

"Why are you crying? It'll work out, Blaze, I promise. I know it seems strange. Please don't let it upset you. Anyone would feel the same as you if they endured what you just have."

She raised her head. "You would feel the same way?"

"Well, no. I would be dumbfounded if I had no memory of who I am. But when I glanced upon your face, I would have thought I had been delivered to an angel."

She felt her mouth move into a smile at his sweet words. Engulfed in his arms once more, she let herself relax. He grabbed her hand gently, showing her to the trunks that held all of her clothing.

"I'll wait outside and give you some time to pull yourself together," he told her in a quiet tone with a tender smile on his face. Then he disappeared behind the closed door.

Wow, I must have a lot of clothes. There are at least five large trunks in here. Standing there, staring at the trunks, she tried not be overwhelmed. *Well, they're not labeled. I guess I'll start at one end and work my way through.*

Walking over, Blaze opened the first chest and looked inside. Her mouth hung open and her eyes widened. Colors, rainbows of colors, erupted from the trunk. Pulling out each shade one by one, she looked at the elegant gowns. Blaze feverishly worked her way through the trunks until she found a white dress that looked plain in comparison, but still portrayed elegance and charm. She dropped her robe and nightdress and let them fall to the ground. Putting her arms in the dress above her head, she worked at sliding it down her figure. It was soft and silky against her skin and she noticed it was fashioned from the same fabric as the bed linen. Glancing into the last trunk, she spied small-niched shelves, which held her shoes. She grabbed a pair of small white flats and slid them on. Admiring the shoes, she wiggled her toes and watched the fabric move. *That's better. My feet are warmer already. These things are soft. Feels like silk around my feet and soft rubber on my soles.*

Dress in place, and shoes on her feet, Blaze turned to the door. She heard muffled chuckles and whispered voices. On her toes, she crept across the room, leaned against the door, and listened, but the hall got quiet. *I swear I heard someone laughing and talking. Now, my hearing must be messed up, too.* Shrugging it off and stepping back, she reached for the door when it opened. It was Slaine with a huge smile on his face.

"I always loved you in that dress. It reminds me of our wedding day. Are you still hungry? Arabella was just telling me that lunch was ready."

"Lunch? What time of day is it? Did I really sleep that long?"

"It is mid-day and Arabella has let us in on the mystery of the locked door. You looked as confused as I was, so I asked her about it. She locked it on her way out last night so the staff wouldn't disturb you this morning. I, however, in my distress did what she was trying to prevent."

"I knew you needed your rest, My Lady," Arabella added. "It was the only thing I could think of to help you."

"It's fine. No need to worry." Hand on her stomach, she added, "I would have awoken soon enough. I'm famished. So, did someone say something about lunch?"

They both seem to be watching me. I will have to make sure I act normal as if nothing is wrong. That's going to be a challenge. Her heart skipped a beat and she jumped when Slaine reached over to hold her hand.

She closed her eyes and made an effort not to cringe. Blaze opened her eyes and looked at him as she spoke. "Oh, I'm sorry. I was taken by surprise. I wasn't expecting that."

I know he says we are married, but holding his hand feels wrongfully out of place. I feel like a blind woman in the land of seers, stumbling around unaware of what is going on right in front of my own face. She reached over and held the crook of his arm instead. That seemed to help. He smiled, at least. The three of them, Arabella leading the way, went to the banquet hall for lunch.

At the table, she sat staring into space for a moment as Slaine explained her being gone for a while. Her brain offered nothing helpful. Her eyes met his when she turned to reply.

"I still have no memory of what happened, or why I was gone in the first place. The only thing I can recall is waking up to find three strangers trying to capture me, and that Demarko fellow in the wagon. No matter how hard I try…it's no use. Speaking of which, where is he and what did you do with Mr. Rude and his sons?"

"Well, as for Mr. Harenton and his sons…I was so happy for your return, I paid him handsomely. However, I was extremely agitated about your treatment so I told him that if he ever so much as breathed in this direction, I would have him hanged for his infraction. Demarko is still here in the guest room, for now, until I can figure out what to do with him. I think it's best to keep an eye on him. I'm not sure I entirely trust him. He could be as innocent as you, but he could be faking this whole memory loss and let himself get captured so that he could get close to you."

"I don't think Demarko was in on some conspiracy plan as you say, but after the time I spent with the other three, I wouldn't be surprised if they were. I don't like Mr. Harenton at all. From the moment I first saw him, I got a really bad feeling."

"I think he's just a money-hungry fool. Once he saw you yesterday, he immediately knew he could have plenty of it. You should have seen his face. It was more coin than he had ever saw. Just out of curiosity, why do you trust that Demarko fellow so easily?"

How can I explain it? I know I can't tell him what I feel when he touches me. I can't explain it to myself let alone to someone else. What If I say something he doesn't like and get Demarko hurt, or worse? I'm not sure if he is the jealous type who would take it wrong or if he would listen and be understanding.

"I don't really know. I can't explain it. He was very kind and tried to keep me calm. He never tried anything off color. When we escaped, he was nothing less than a gentleman. When Benjamin tried to put me to sleep with that spell of his that didn't work, Demarko was very worried they had just killed me. Mainly, we just worked together to get free."

"Wait! What do you mean *tried*? Mr. Shaunt informed me he had put you to sleep. He'll be pleased to hear otherwise. He does worry. I forbid magic in this part of the country, especially to use it on the Queen herself. If I hadn't been so happy to see you, I would have killed them all starting with the mage!"

"What I mean is just what I said…*tried*. I faked it to test them. I wasn't sure what they were capable of, or what they were up to, so I pretended to be asleep in hopes they would talk or something. Nothing, of course, happened. They were completely quiet. As I said, Demarko yelled at them, demanding to know what they had done. He was genuinely upset about it. After he was quiet, I opened my eyes and looked at him to let him know I was okay. We rode the rest of the way like that."

"Remarkable! You are one brilliant woman, which is why I love you. You had no idea what was going on, who you were, or where you were going, and still tried to take on three not so small men. Bound and tied even, and still…"

He looks amazed by that statement. Oh, dear, I think I'm blushing. "It was nothing special…just plain ole survival instincts."

She glanced over and saw him looking at her as if he had never seen her before today. "What?"

"Nothing. You just amaze me, that's all."

Well, this is just odd. I can't put my finger on it, but he's strange. Maybe it's his eyes that chill my spine. Well, sounds like Arabella with the food. I'm glad for the interruption. Good God, she and the staff have enough food to feed an army.

"Are we having guests?"

The food was carried on huge crystal platters and was packed with everything one could think of. They had bacon, eggs, sausage, roasted quail, and even fresh baked bread accompanied by large crystal pitchers filled with wine, ale, and juice.

"No guests, my dear, just us. I made them cook just about everything. I wasn't sure of what you would be hungry for."

"Why not just ask me what I'm in the mood for? Of course at this point, as hungry as I am, I could eat anything." Stomach growling and her mouth watering, she eyed all the food, trying to figure out what she would eat first.

"Well, I guess that would have been a wise decision."

"I apologize that I have hurt your feelings again. That came out wrong. Let me start over... Thank you. This is very thoughtful."

"Blaze, you don't have to apologize. I was trying to help, and you're right, I should have asked. It might have saved the staff from cooking all night."

"I think I will have bacon and eggs."

Her voice joined with Demarko's as he entered the room, sounding even sweeter. *Now, that goes together. My voice and his. Why is that? Why is Slaine so different?*

Glancing at Demarko, she quickly started shoveling her mouth full of food in hopes Slaine wouldn't ask questions. Watching Slaine out of the corner of her eye and quickly shooting glances at Demarko, she saw him bow before them. Blaze noticed Slaine to her left, anger clearly etched in his features. *Oh, this is going to be interesting. What's his problem, anyway? It's not as if we planned it out just to make him mad.* After a moment of silence, Demarko walked over to the other tables, sat down, and waited quietly. She saw Slaine take a couple of quick breaths and fix his expression before he spoke.

"Demarko, why don't you join us for lunch?"

"Thank you, My Lord, it's no trouble. I don't mind coming back later when you and the Queen are finished. When I first entered the room, I didn't know you were both here. I was overcome with the delicious aroma and spoke aloud, not meaning to."

Unable to control herself, she let her mouth open and her voice fill the air. "Nonsense. You may join us. There's so much food, we may have to invite the army just to help eat it all."

Hoping to soften his mood, she smiled at Slaine as she

motioned for Demarko to have a seat. *I was starving, but now I'm not sure I can eat. My stomach is knotting up. It definitely promises to be an interesting meal.*

The fine hairs on her arms and the back of her neck rose, the room felt so tense. Fork in hand, she picked at her food while she watched the men at the table. Slaine dryly ate his lunch and Demarko looked up several times as he attempted to eat. The staff had left the three of them alone. *This room is so quiet, if someone coughed right now, I bet it would bounce off these walls like an explosion. How do I fix it?*

A quick movement to her left caught her attention. Slaine had stood. She turned in his direction and he grabbed her hand, kissed it once, and left the room. After hearing his footfalls disappear, she sighed deeply, letting herself relax. *That was intense. I'm glad he left.*

Blaze quickly glanced behind her, checking that he had gone before she went back to her meal. The room had been so quiet and tense that she jumped when Demarko spoke.

"Did you sleep well, My Lady? The whole castle seems as worried as the King, which is as it should be. I was in my room this morning and the maid staff was asking me all kinds of questions—if I was really with you, were you okay, and the one question we don't have an answer for..."

"What happened?" they both said together and laughed.

Caught up in her conversation with Demarko, she didn't notice Arabella had re-entered and walked toward the table.

"What is this? Is this the first sign the Queen is getting better after all? That's twice today the two of you seem be thinking the same thing. Hmm makes one curious..." Snickering, she added "Don't worry. I won't tell anyone as to why the whole town might start talking."

She watched the woman finish refilling their glasses and walk off smiling and humming to herself.

"I like her—a bit off, but I think that might be what I like about her the most."

"She seems very sweet and at the same time, mischievous. I like her, too! So, what are your plans, now? Do you have any? You may stay here as long as you would like. With no memory, how do you know what to do?" Lifting her head, she looked at him as she waited for his answer.

"Plans, I'm not sure. I'm also unsure that staying here in the castle is a good idea either. I was actually thinking I would go to the village and see if I could find some work, perhaps stay at that fancy inn I keep hearing about. The only problem I see is I'm not able to remember what skills I have. I'm positive that I have some, but I just don't remember them."

"Then it's settled. You have no choice but to stay until we—I mean *you* can figure out what it is you can do. I won't allow you to leave the castle and go out into the village devoid of gold, a home, or a means of work. We have plenty of room here and you probably won't get food as good as Arabella's if you stayed at the Inn Dever. It doesn't seem right to have you leave under these circumstances. You'll stay here, please. I'll help in any way I can."

Her mind soon raced ahead. *What is wrong with me? He's not my husband and King, but the thought of him leaving is sending me headlong into panic mode.* Heart beating faster, and lungs pulling uneven breaths, she had to concentrate in order to keep herself under control.

Settling down, she focused on her dilemma. *I'm just worried for him, that's all. I don't want to see anyone uncared for.* Her brain mapped out a rational response, but her heart inferred a different point. *I'm so confused. If I could just figure this out. I think I'm going to be sick.* Clearing her throat with the intention of excusing herself, she found her gaze meeting his and she felt her body lower back into the seat. He picked up the conversation where she had left off.

Chapter Five
Castle and Garden

Blaze retired to her room after dinner. Again, it was more of a feast than an actual dinner. It had been the three of them once more and again she noticed Slaine's agitation. Unable to tell, she asked him about it.

"Are you okay…you seem reserved?"

"I'm fine."

She paid attention to his body language as he spoke. *Wow, his hair doesn't even move when he shakes his head from side to side. I wonder how he does that.*

"Blaze, I'm sorry. I have missed you and I was hoping to have all of your attention. I understand that as King and Queen we have obligations we must address. "

"You seem like you don't want us to help Demarko, but what are we to do? We can't make him leave. How's he to work and live?"

"No, I know. I'm glad that he has decided to stay at the castle and Shaunt has agreed to help him get him back on his feet."

When she looked at him and smiled, it seemed to soften his mood some. They had reached her bedchamber door when he turned to her and asked, "Would you like for me to stay with you?"

"That won't be necessary, but thank you."

"I understand. Goodnight, then."

"Goodnight." She watched him walk away down the hall before

opening her door and entering her room. With her back against the wooden frame after she closed it, she became aware her heart felt very heavy and her mind seemed more troubled.

I hope he truly understands. I'm not trying to hurt his feelings or dash his hopes. I just don't feel anything for him. For me, it's as if I don't know him. I don't know anything of my past, but I'm pretty darn sure I was never able to just fall into bed with someone. It just doesn't feel right.

Blaze strolled through her room, running her fingers gently across her possessions, hoping to spark something—a memory, a flash of recognition, but nothing surfaced. Turning toward the bookshelf, head tilted to the side, reading the many titles, she heard a soft knock at the door. Moving her head to its normal position and turning on her heels, she faced the door and spoke.

"You may enter." The door opened and Arabella quickly entered and closed the door behind her.

"My Lady, I brought you some tea. Would you like me to prepare the bathing room and fluff your bed?"

"I would like some tea, thank you. Can we talk? I could use a friend. You *did* say we're friends. It seems as though I can trust you."

"Come, my dear."

She let Arabella escort her to the divan. She took the tea and watched the woman set the tray on the nearest table before sitting down herself.

"What would you like to talk about?"

Sitting on the edge of the seat, back straight, she took a small sip before she let her fears and questions spill out.

"I don't remember anything at all. I'm so surprised at the fact I know my own name. I'm trying to search my brain and it's as blank as parchment, only filling in what I'm doing at the present. I have some feeling as to what is real, like the fact I'm Queen. When I was told I was Queen, at first, it was a shock, but then it seemed to fit. When you mentioned we were friends, I sensed that was true. Some things in this castle seem familiar, but others don't. Please don't repeat this last part, but the fact that Slaine is King and that we are married just doesn't fit. It's like a puzzle piece that looks as though it fits in with the picture, but does not fit the shape. No matter how hard you press and turn it, it just isn't going to fit. I'm horrible, I know, for not knowing my own husband, but I can't make myself feel anything for him. I look at him, and yes, he is handsome, but there is something off. I fear that I'm doing something wrong. It's so frustrating. What can I do?"

"First, my dear, you can start drinking that tea and calming those over-worked nerves of yours. Now, don't feel bad for forgetting. It's not something that you do at will, or have any control over. As for the familiar and not so familiar, that will come in time. Don't fret over it too much. Trying too hard may keep those memories from surfacing sooner. Just breathe and take it easy and it'll come to you. I don't believe this is permanent. I'm not sure what has happened, but I'm certain that it'll pass in time. As for My Lord, the King, just follow your instincts and it will always lead you in the right direction. Your true love will find his way back into your heart."

Sipping her tea and listening to Arabella, Blaze focused on calming her nerves and allowed the woman to comfort her. Her eyes watched the woman as she spoke and she nodded once or twice and asked another question.

"What do I do?"

"I just told you, my dear."

"No. I heard you about that and I will take your advice. I meant, what are my duties around here in the castle? I don't remember my daily activities. I assume there is plenty of castle business to handle. This is a big place and I'm sure I don't just sit around and look pretty all day."

"Well, first, looking pretty was never anything you ever had to *work* at, nor did it mean as much to you as others. You have many duties. Are you certain you want to get back to those so quickly? You need to rest."

Taking the tea from her lips, she opened her mouth and Arabella held a hand up and continued.

"If you would like, tomorrow, we can start by getting you

reacquainted with the castle grounds. Perhaps it will help your memory. As for right now, it's getting late and as I said, you need rest. I'll see you in the morning."

Cup back to her lips, she sipped it once and smiled around the rim at the prospect of getting back to normal. *I hope that this will help and people will stop staring at me. I feel like a carnival act walking the halls.* She reached out her hand and touched Arabella's arm.

"Wait, before you go. Where will you be? Can I meet you in the banquet hall?"

"That would be fine, dear. After breakfast, we can walk the castle grounds. Your memory's already on the mend. You have been referring to the throne room as the banquet hall just as you always have. You never spent much time sitting in that throne. You always preferred to be down at the table with the townies. You only use the throne for official business. That's why I have always admired you, Blaze. You were never one to flaunt your power over others. You love being with the townspeople. Maybe, once you are familiar with the castle, we can go for a walk in town. That would make the townspeople happy to see that you are getting well. They do worry so."

"Thank you, Arabella I would love that. I think getting back to some normalcy will help me out a lot. You are a real gem."

She watched the woman hustle out of the room and close the door, leaving only the quiet behind. Huddled on the couch, knees bent and covered by her dress, she sipped her tea and felt her body relax. Her eyes drooped, her mouth opened, and she yawned. *It has been a tiring day. I need to get some sleep. Big day tomorrow.* Leaning forward, she set the cup on the small stand and headed for bed. Head on soft pillows, blankets warm and gathered close, her eyes closed, and the young couple from the night before crept back into her dreams...

"These are for you. I hope you like them."
Flowers in hand she raised them to her face, smelled the sweet aroma, and smiled. "I love them! Thank you. How did you know

Pedalstem Lillies were my favorite?" He glanced over his shoulder, then back at her and she knew where he got his information. Arabella!

"Would you believe, lucky guess?"

"No, but I love them anyway."

She took the arm he extended and dropped the bouquet on the table, then they walked out of the castle and into the cool fall air.

"Where should we go first?"

"Well, Kipper and Kamron should be up soon in the sword fight tournament. Let's start there."

"Sword fighting it is."

Cool air on her right side, the warmth from his body on her left and an electric current running through her veins, she eyed the fighters as they entered the arena. Eyes glued on the action, she watched as Kipper took down his opponent. Swinging widely from left to right, he blocked the strikes. His opponent paused and Kipper took his opening shot. Hitting him with his shield in his left hand, he knocked the mock enemy off balance. Kipper slid his leg out, tripping the man, and placed the tip of his sword at his throat.

Jumping to her feet, clapping her hands, she cheered loudly with the crowd as they announced Kipper as the winner. "He's really good."

"Yes, he is. I have seen him and Kamron practicing in the stable arena. They both are very good."

"Oh, look, it's Kamron's turn."

Her hands on her lower back, she flattened her dress against her legs and sat down. Leaning into Woody, she got comfortable and watched Kamron's performance. His match was over quickly, too. Swinging quick and deliberate, he forced the mock enemy back, inch by inch until his back was against the wall. Raising his shield, he faked a swing with the left hand and brought up the butt of his sword with his right, backhanding the man into unconsciousness. Another winner. Joining the crowd, she yelled and cheered for her friend's victory.

"Do you want to go get some hot spiced tea? It's a bit chilly *out."*

"Yes. Should we go and say hello to the twins?"

"Not now. They will be collecting their rewards and getting ready for the challenges tomorrow. They are working their way up the ranks. Two more wins, like today, and they are likely to be fighting each other in the finals."

"Well, in that case, let's go get something hot to drink. I'm getting a cold."

Her fingers entwined with his, she let him lead the way to the tea station.

With a hay bale beneath her, she sipped her hot tea and watched two dare devils juggle, toss, and swallow flaming torches and swords.

"Are you having a good time?"

Blaze pulled her eyes from the pyrotechnics and looked at him. "Yes, I am. Thank you."

"Good. I'm glad. Are you still cold? We could go back if you want."

"No, I'm fine. Between this hot tea and you, I'm plenty warm."

Eyes locked on his, her hands cupped in his, her breathing stopped and her heart raced. His eyes are so beautiful. So bright, they almost sparkle. *Shadows crossed her frame blocking the light from the sun. She looked over and saw two people standing in front of her—two dark haired boys, one taller than the other. As she stared at the two young boys, the skinny one spoke first.*

"Hello. So, how do you like the festival? Nice, huh?"

"Yes. Who are you? I'm sorry, but do I know you?"

"Well, you should, but you don't. They call me Slim and we call him D."

Slim and D? She leaned her frame into Woody's and whispered in his ear. "Do you know them?"

"No."

"So, anyway, my parents own the Inn Dever...that fancy black and red building over there. We house some of the wealthiest dignitaries around. Why, right now, the inn is full because of the festival. So, exactly who are you?"

"My friends call me Red. Nice to me—"

Stopping in mid-sentence, and dropping the smile from her face, she glared at the skinny boy, trying to figure out why he stopped her from talking.

"We know who you are...The Princess. I was referring to the hound next to you."

Oh, you keep on laughing. Who do they think they are? *Blaze twisted her frame and glanced all the way around her, feigning to be looking for something. "Where is a dog? I don't see a dog?"*

"Are you blind? He is sitting right next to you."

As smug smiles crossed their features, her stomach rolled with disgust. I don't think I like these boys. I hate arrogant attitudes. *"He's no hound. This is my boyfriend. We call him Woody."*

"Woody, is it? What kind of name is Woody, anyway?"

"Is that some kind of bird or something?" D asked.

She sat up squaring her shoulders and glared at the two boys. "You know, I really don't like your attitudes."

Before she could say anything else, Woody interjected and stopped her. He tugged softly on her arm and she looked in his face when he spoke.

"How about we go get some more tea?"

"Yes, that sounds nice. Afterwards, we can huddle close while we watch the jousting match."

Hands on her knees, she stood at the same time as Woody. Her arm looped through his and she glanced at the we're-better-than-you expression on the other boy's faces and walked away. Body heat radiated from him as she wrapped her arm around his waist and put her thumb through one of the loops on his pants. They walked for a few minutes, enjoying the silence when he turned to ask a question.

"Did you know you are very cute when you are angry?"

She turned to face him. "Thank you, and I'm sorry. I hate when people act that way. That kind of behavior only makes them look petty and stupid."

"I agree. Did you mean what you said...you know, about me being your boyfriend, or was that just for their benefit? Is that

what you want?"

Mouth dry, heart stuck in her throat, sweat beading her brow, she couldn't speak. Oh, no, she thought—I have opened my mouth and now he is wondering about it. Great. I have ruined things. Too fast. What should I say? What would repair this disaster? Should I just say yes?

Her eyes stared into his. She felt one of his hands on her shoulder, the other on her face and still she couldn't speak.

"I would like for it to be true," he said. "Please say something. Are you okay?"

"Y...yes."

"Yes...what? Yes to being my girlfriend, or yes, you are okay?"

"B—both."

Her breathing came back, her heart slowed, and her body slumped in relaxation. Oh, how I love his smile. Whew. What did I expect him to say? Should have known that would be what he wanted. He did kiss me earlier. I'm being foolish. All that sweating for nothing. *Arms crossed onto her chest, she leaned into him when he hugged her, cradling her body in his arms. She pushed him slightly away and looked at him.*

"So, boyfriend, how about we go back to the castle now. It has gotten colder than I expected it to."

"As you wish."

Hands folded over her arms, shivering slightly, she felt the surge of electricity run through her when he reached over and wrapped her in his embrace. I love it when he touches me. His body heat plus electricity...can it get any better than that?

She stepped out of his embrace long enough to walk through the castle doors. Engaged in conversation and back in his hold, she didn't notice her father sitting at the head table until he spoke.

"Red, Woody, did you enjoy the festival?"

She jumped. Her face reddened. She hid her hands behind her, stepped out of Woody's arms, and smiled innocently at father. "Yes, Father. We had a great time. Woody was a perfect gentleman. Although we did meet two boys earlier, they were strange. Other than that, no major disasters. "

She watched her father as she spoke and knew right away that what she'd said alarmed him. His face changed color and he leaned forward.

"What do you mean strange? What happened? Woody, would you explain it to me, please?"

"Nothing happened, sir. That skinny boy, Slim and his brother D got rude and Miss Brilliant here told them what she thought about it. Then we walked away. I assure you, King Alexander, I wouldn't have let anyone lay a finger on her if that's your worry."

"I'm certain that my daughter would be fully protected with you in her company. That's the only reason you two went alone in the first place. I just wanted to be positive it wasn't something I needed to look into."

"No need to be alarmed, My Lord."

Movement from the left caught her attention. She turned to see her mother who walked into the room and stood by her father. Exchanging glances with her, she smiled back at her.

"Kathryn, dear, why don't you walk Red to her room and see that she is settled for the night. I would like to talk to young Woody."

"I was already planning on it. I want to hear all about her evening."

She's going to want all the details. She always does. *Her eyes rolling at her parents' expressions, she turned to Woody and bid him goodnight.*

"Thank You. I had a wonderful time. I'll see you tomorrow."

"I had fun, too. Thank you for accompanying me...sweet dreams."

"That's enough, you two. Now, it's my turn."

Her mother's arm around her shoulder, turning her away from Woody, she led her toward her room. Blaze leaned against her, laughed, and waited for the inquisition to start.

"So, tell me about it. Was he a gentleman? What did you do? Do you think the flowers were a lucky guess, or did someone tip him off?

Her heart still beating quickly, her breathing uneven, and her head a bit dizzy, she felt euphoric. Walking side by side, they started up the stairs as she answered her mother's questions.

"I had a great time. He was more than a gentleman. Yes, I know Arabella tipped him off. We walked around and watched the twins in their match. They won, by the way. My heart just about fell through my chest when we watched the men playing with fire. We had spiced tea and he asked me if I wanted to be his girlfriend. That's the whole of it."

"I'm glad that you had a good time and that you decided to go with Woody. He's a nice boy."

Hand working the latch, she opened the door to her room. As she walked in, she waited for her mother to enter and closed the door behind her. Head still in the clouds, she floated to her wardrobe and changed into her nightdress. With her dress hung neatly in the armoire and after closing the wooden door, she looked over to see her mother sitting on her bed. She climbed on the bed next to her, stretched out, and faced her so they could finish their chat.

"So? What did you say?"

"To what?"

"You said he asked you to be his girlfriend? What did you say?"

"Oh, I said yes, of course." Falling onto her back, she stared at the ceiling for a split second before rolling back onto her side. She could feel the heat in her face and a wide smile on her lips.

"He's so handsome. I almost fainted when we were talking about it."

"So, you like him, then?"

Burying her face in the blankets, she laughed aloud. "Yes, I like him. There is something there. Between us, I mean...I feel...I don't know how to explain it."

"Well, give it your best shot. I'm almost bursting at the seams here. I'm so happy!"

When she glanced in her mother's direction, she couldn't help but smile. Her face reflected the same excited happiness she felt. Electric currents still ran through her, only this time, giddy giggling happiness caused it.

"Earlier, behind the kitchen, he kissed me."

"He did what? Never mind...finish the story. I want to hear this."

If she weren't still smiling, I would think I was in trouble. *"Please don't be mad. I have to tell you this. It was incredible. And I'm a little confused."*

"I'm not mad. I was just a little shocked. What are you confused about?"

She sat up and got serious. Holding the pillows in her lap, she took a deep breath. "Well, like I said, it was wonderful. There is some kind of connection, though, I think. When we were kissing...well...I could feel everything."

"Sweetie, you are supposed to feel everything. That is, you are supposed to feel what he's doing, anyway, and if not, he isn't doing it right."

"That's not what I meant. I mean, I felt all that and everything else. I could feel his hands on my waist. I could feel him kissing me, and the warmth from his body pressed into mine. I could also feel the grass through my shoes, the sun and air across my skin and...electricity."

She studied her mother's face and waited to see confusion or disbelief. Instead, she got a wide smile. Huh? Why is she smiling? I didn't think her smile could get any bigger. Why is she softly clapping? She looks like a schoolgirl if that is even possible.

"Mother? Why are you smiling? I'm being serious. This isn't a joke."

"I know. I know. I'm just so happy for you."

"So...is that normal?"

"Not for most people, but for you, yes."

"What does that...who could that be?"

Exhaling in frustration, she slid off the bed and went to open the door. Latch lifted, she pulled it open and couldn't help but smile back at her father's broad smile.

"Hello, Father."

Standing on her tiptoes, she reached up and hugged him. "Did you play nice with Woody?"

"Well, of course. He's growing into a fine man. Just like his father. He comes from good stock...fine family."

Blaze looked at his smiling face and shot him a smile laced with a suspicious look. *"Father, would you still think he came from good stock if his parents weren't your best friends?"*

Her eyes on his towering frame, she watched him fidget and his face change color slightly before he cleared his throat and spoke.

"Wh—ye—Yes. Yes, I think I would. Although it does score some extra points for the lad that he's my best friend's son."

Her smile broke her serious facade and she joined in her parent's laughter.

Her mother broke the laughter first. *"I hope you didn't come down too hard on the boy. Did you give him the same speech my father gave you?"*

"Good Lord, no. That boy might not have the nerves I do. He might have turned tail and run for the hills. Good as gold, I promise. Red, I have to say I approve."

I know that look. He is up to something. She is, too. It's written all over their faces. Do they think they are hiding anything giving each other those looks? *Her hands thrown in the air for a second, she looked at both of her parent's faces and tried to put on her best serious expression. She concentrated hard in order to keep from breaking into a smile at the expressions her parents were giving her. She was never good with serious looks.*

"What is going on? What are you two up to?"

"Who? Us?" they said in unison.

"Yes, you."

Staring at her parents, it was hard not to laugh. They looked like children caught with their hands in the candy jar. They both had hurt expression on their faces, hands over their hearts and smiles twitching at the side of their mouths.

"You two look guilty."

She placed her arms over her chest, tapped her foot, and glared at them. Her breathing, her parents' breathing, and the wick burning on the candle, seemed the only sound in the room. Her façade was broken along with her silence, when her father's booming laughter echoed off the walls. Laughter escaped her and a smile crossed her face as she looked at her father bent over almost busting the buttons on his shirt from the strain.

"What's so funny?"

"That hasn't worked since you were little."

"What hasn't worked?"

"That right there. Your temper stance."

"My what?"

"That's the exact pose you struck when you didn't get your way when you were younger. Your father always thought it was so cute, he would cave and give you what you wanted," her mother informed her.

"Oh, so why isn't it working now?"

"Well, because...no offence, Princess, but it just...well, you can't really pull off the serious look. It doesn't fit your face. It's not you, well, not you when you're really not mad anyway," her father explained.

"What he's trying to say is, when you're not really mad, your serious face is...well it looks like a cross between a frown and a smile," her mother said.

"You're right. I'm not mad. But I know you two are up to something."

"Nooo, we are just happy for you, that's all."

She turned to her mother since her father's laughter left him helpless just then. "Ah-huh. Fine...subject change. You were saying earlier that it was normal for me. What did you mean?"

"You have had a busy evening. You need to get some sleep. We'll talk more at a later time."

Her body squished in a bear hug by her father and a soft embrace from her mother, she hugged them back and dropped the subject. Hug over, she stepped back and took a deep breath.

"I know you're up to something, but I'm going to drop it for now. I'm tired. I love you."

"We love you, too."

Wet kisses on her cheek, she walked them out. She stood with her hand on the open door and smiled as she watched them walk arm in arm down the hallway and the stairs. No wonder they get along so well, she thought. They both like to aggravate me. I hope Woody and I have children we can aggravate one day.

* * * *

The door opened and the warm smell of hot food filled the air. Demarko's mouth watered and his stomach growled. "I'll have some bacon and eggs again today."

His heart leapt with joy at hearing her voice mixed with his. Demarko's gaze went to the front of the room. She sat at the table staring back at him, the King by her side. Unsuccessful at getting out of breakfast, he joined them. His skin crawled and his muscles flexed, feeling the tension in the room. With his elbows slightly off the table and fork in hand, he took small bites between questions. Gazing at her, returning her smile, he pushed the plate away and finished their conversation after King Deverox left. *She's so beautiful...her face, her body, her demeanor, and even her laugh. Why must she beg me to stay? It's hard enough to think about not staying close. I fear for her. The King's facade of happiness slipped twice in the short time he was here. Moreover, the look that flickered across his face wasn't one of fear or even anger. It was hate or maybe rage. Either way I hope she never sees it. I just wish I knew what was going on and how to remedy it.*

"My Lady, if you will excuse me, I think I'm going to get some fresh air. Is that alright?"

"Yes, of course. I'm just about finished with breakfast and Arabella is going to give me a tour of the castle. We're hoping it jogs my memory. "

"I hope it's successful. Now, if you'll excuse me, I hear sunshine calling my name. Good day, My Lady."

He pushed away from the table, bowed once, smiled at her, and walked away. He focused his mind on what lay beyond the castle doors.

Fresh air filled his lungs, the warmth of the sun's rays played across his skin and a small breeze blew through his hair. *What a beautiful day. Not hot and not cold. Perfect. Now, down to the village to see about work.* Sunshine on his face, he strode down the hill toward the village and a familiar voice caught his attention.

"Good to see you up and around. Feeling better?"

"Yes, thank you. I was just going for a walk, Mr. Shaunt. Would you care to join me?"

"Don't mind if I do, thank you."

He walked briskly with Shaunt next to him and explained the conversation he had during breakfast.

"I don't feel comfortable in the castle. I get the feeling the King would rather I not be here. At the same time, she is right, but I'm sure I can manage. You should have seen the look on her face when I talked of leaving. I don't know what I'm going to do. No matter what I choose, I'll be upsetting one of them. Any advice?"

His aggravation level seemed to rise with each question he couldn't answer. He felt the man's hand on his shoulder. He stooped and turned to face him.

"Actually, I do. How about you come and stay at the stablehand quarters. You could help me out. I'm short a man. It'll keep you out of the King's way, which will please him, yet close enough that the Queen won't worry so. "

Air escaped through his lungs as he sighed with relief. His mind stopped racing, his shoulders felt lighter and his heart beat even once more.

"That is wonderful. I'll take it."

"Well, come on then. I'll show you to the stables."

The smell of wet dirt, hay, and manure filled his nose and crawled across his tongue. His jaw moved from side to side as he worked up saliva and tried to swallow the taste away. The stomping of hooves, neighing of horses, the shuffling of feet, and the scraping of tools across ground filled the area. Demarko watched men with wheelbarrows, shovels, and rakes moving working and yelling commands as they darted from one space to another. *This stable looks to be as big as the castle. I wonder how many horses are in here.* He stood next to the large wooden doors and scanned the inside of enclosure. The walls were tall and crossed with large beams along the roof. Saddles, and tack and gear hung from oversized nails or sat upon huge shelves lining the inside hall. The massive heads of horses bobbed in and out of stall windows in different shades, being nosy and wanting attention. His eyes scanned from right to left as he watched the commotion. The sound of Shaunt's voice in his ear caused him to look away.

"It's not much, but you may stay as long as you like."

"It'll be fine. Thank you."

"I hope that you and the Queen are both better soon."

He turned toward the man, reached out and shook Shaunt's hand. Keeping his gaze on the magistrate, he put on a big smile and spoke.

"I hope so, too. I'm not sure anyone believes me, but I truly can't remember anything. To be honest, the only reason I said my name was Demarko was that it sounded right. I'm not sure of anything. My mind is so fuzzy. I just don't remember anything at all."

"True enough. That makes twice you have said that same thing…" Shaunt said. Chuckling, he added, "Must not have remembered the first." Patting Demarko on the shoulder, he added, "I'm positive it'll all come flooding back soon enough. Here, let me show you your room—it's just up the stairs."

His feet shuffled as he slowly followed Shaunt around the corner and up the stairs. On the landing, he stopped for only a moment and waited as Shaunt opened the door. He stepped around Shaunt's frame and took in each part of the room as Shaunt pointed it out.

"Anyway here's the bed, and over there is the wash basin. I'll expect you ready and at my desk at sunrise."

"I'll be there. Thank you again."

"Anytime. Besides, you're really the one helping me. Keeps me from having to go into town and recruit. Get settled and if you need anything, the guards and workers will be more than willing to help you out."

Demarko shook Shaunt's hand one last time and closed the door when he left the room. Leaning back on the door, he scanned the small room and smiled. *It's perfect...small and simple.* The bed was freshly made, nestled in the center of the room, and covered with a large fur. One small table holding an oil lamp within arm's reach sat next to the bed. A large trunk sat next to the door. The washbasin built into the frame sat next to the only window across the room. In three strides, he crossed the small area. His hand on the window sill, he looked past the castle grounds and into the small village.

Look at all those people shuffling from here to there working and caring for their families. All of them have knowledge and memories of who they are. The men pulling wagons of iron and goods remember where and to whom each load is destined. The women carrying children and food stores know each precious face and know how much it will take to feed that child. Wait! What is this? Is that... It is. He looks angry. I wonder who they are looking for. Apparently, they didn't find who they were looking for at the...Inn Dever. That's where I was heading before Shaunt stopped me. Is he looking for me? Surely not. I'm just being paranoid.

Demarko watched the scene through the window and saw King Deverox with a battalion of Elite Guards walk back toward the castle. Air escaping his lungs, he dropped his hand and his gaze, then went to sit on the bed. The corner of the mattress nearly touched the floor from his weight as he sat down and took off his boots. He slid them to the side and scooted toward the head of the mattress. *This bed isn't' bad. It's almost as comfortable as the one in the guest rooms.* The cool wall pressed against his back, the softness of the mattress gave way and he sank a little as he lay back and stretched out. Legs crossed at the ankles, arms folded behind his head, he stared into the ceiling. *I can cross finding work and a roof over my head off my long list of things to figure out. At least that was something I could control and do. Memories, past life, and who I am...one day at a time, I guess. Having a plan makes me feel better.* Reaching out, his hands closed over the softness of the pillow, he leaned over, rested his head and a young man entered his dream…

Woody stood at the closed door waiting for her to open it and invite him in. He turned his head left and right checking the hall to be sure he was alone. A smile plastered on his face, he heard her footsteps and the creaking of the door swing open.

"What are you doing here? My father might change his mind about you if he catches you.

Quietly, he stepped into the room, engulfed her in his arms and closed the door with a swing of his leg. He stared down at her smiling face and he couldn't help but smile himself as he kissed her. He pulled away, prepared to speak, and noticed her breathing now just as ragged as his. His body and mind filled with excitement. His heart beat faster, his pulse raced, and heat swam along his nerves just below his skin.

"I don't think he'll catch me. I watched your parents leave, arm in arm, whispering and laughing. About us, I'm positive. My parents are acting the same way. I didn't get a chance to say goodnight, properly. Plus, I wanted to make sure I would see you tomorrow, but I could leave if you want."

"No, that's fine. You're already here. As to whether or not you will see me…we do live in the same castle. I'm sure we're bound to run into one another."

"That is not what I meant and you know it. So, will you attend the rest of the festival with me and allow me to escort you to the Fall Feast?"

"Well, I suppose I can. I mean, I have to go with someone, so it might as well be you. However, there is one condition."

"And what would that be?"

"You have to bring me more of those lilies."

"Oh, is that all? Here I thought you might ask for something hard."

Heat, electricity, and lust took hold. He wrapped her in his arms, kissed her, and carried her to the bed. Arms on either side of her frame, he tried to pull away. Not here. I have to stop this. *His body entwined with hers and the blankets and he continued to kiss patterns onto her neck and ears. The alarm in her voice stopped him cold.*

"Wait. You have to stop now. I'm afraid if this continues, we're going to get caught and my father won't care that you're his best friend's son."

"I'm perfectly fine with that, but you're the one who started it this time. I tried to pull away and stop it. You're the one who got us all bound up in the sheets."

"I know. I just...never mind."

Pulling and jerking on the blankets, he unraveled himself and moved off the bed. He took a few deep breaths, trying to calm his nerves and his lust. He watched her sit up and do the same. Her hair seemed a bird's nest. Her face was pink and flushed, her skin red and blotchy, and her nightdress on one side drooped down, exposing the top of her breast. A few more moans in my ear and I'm not sure we would have stopped.

"Woody, would you please button your shirt. It's...you know. In case someone walks in, I don't want them to think..."

"Not a bad idea. You should probably fix your dress. Well, as best you can. Somehow, your strap broke. Looking like that...you saying no is the only reason I'm still on this side of the bed. You're right. I need to go. "

He watched as Red looked into the bedside mirror and checked her appearance. She tried to use her fingers to restrain her hair. She finally gave up and covered herself with her blankets. Closing his eyes and taking a deep breath, he ran his fingers through his own hair and turned to walk out. If I don't get out of here soon and she happens to touch me...we're done for, and I'm a dead man.

"Wait. Can I ask you a question?"

Turning to face her, he asked, "What do you want to know?"

"Sit back down. What exactly did my father say to you?"

As he sat on the far end of the bed, he made sure he put plenty of distance between them. Glad she covered herself, he looked at her and answered her question.

"Just...you know...father to guy stuff. Why?"

"I just wanted to know, and no, I don't know."

"It doesn't matter, but if you must know…"

"Yes, I must know. I'm completely curious. He left here glowing and talking cryptic. He refused to explain it."

"He was smiling because he knows what we do."

"And that would be?"

"That we are crazy about each other and we are meant to be together."

"Ah-huh. What exactly did you tell him?"

"Only what he wanted to know."

"You're making me crazy."

"I told him the same as I did last year when we went to the festival the first time. Remember? He asked if we could talk. My answer is still the same."

"And you said?"

"I love you. We are meant for one another and they know it as well as we do. We have a connection and have always had. There is something there, and I know you feel it, too."

"Thank God. I thought it was just me. When I asked my mother about it last year, she said it wasn't normal for everybody, but it was normal for me. She never explained what she meant, but I'm glad you felt it, too."

"How could I not? I crave just to be next to you, to hear your voice. I always have. I just never understood it and I still don't. Well, you know what that's like."

"I think my dress and your shirt prove I know how you felt. It is almost like…a pull of some kind."

"Then you know I'm telling the truth when I say that I love you."

"I love you, too."

Before he could blink, his body lay flat on the bed with her atop of him, kissing. His shirt lay crumpled on the floor and her nightdress was gathered around her waist. His hands on her hips, he rolled her onto her back, and her legs encircled him. His mouth moved with hers, his hair wound in knots by her hands. His breathing was heavy, his heart was racing, and he felt his self-control slipping. *He felt her hands move down his spine and to his waist. His eyes opened, and shock overwhelmed him when she slipped her hands over the seam of pants.* Oh, Lord, we are going to be caught. *He grabbed her hands and gently moved away.*

"*We have to stop this. You're right. We are going to get caught. Do you realize how loud we were getting? We just got started. We will just have to wait until we're alone.*"

"*You're right. I got carried away. I'm sorry.*"

"*Let's not be sorry. Let's be smart and careful.*" *He reached down and grabbed his shirt from the floor. Putting it on, he glanced at her once more.* Don't touch her. Just say goodbye.

"*Sweet dreams. I'll see you in the morning. I love you, My Lady Red.*"

"*I love you, too. I think it would be wise if we say we have had our goodnight kiss and you just leave. I'm afraid that if you get close, we'll finish it.*"

"*I agree with that. Wise decision. Goodnight.*"

He heard her goodnight as he walked out the door. Closing the door quietly behind him, he looked both ways and hurried away to dunk himself in the water barrel.

The sun coming through the open window mixed with shadows, causing a striped pattern of light and dark to fan across the room. Breathing deeply, Demarko cleared his lungs and looked around. *Sunrise? No, high noon. Where...right stables, top of the stairs.* Shaking his head and rubbing his eyes, he tried to push past the memory of his dream. A little disoriented, he slid off the bed and walked to the washbasin to wash away the sleepiness. *It was so real. I could feel the softness of her skin, the warmth of her desire, and smell of her perfume. Do I know her? She looked...almost familiar.* Hands cupped with water, he splashed his face. *I must have a vivid imagination.*

Cool air brushing the damp skin on his face felt refreshing. Small towel in hand, he patted his skin dry. Setting the towel on the edge of the sink, he looked down and noticed he still wore his clothes. *Well, at least I don't have to get dressed. I need to hurry.*

My first day on the job and I'm late. Great!

Quickly rushing to the bed, he flopped down and worked his feet into his boots. Jumping up, he hurried to the door. He flung it open, then shut it and rushed down the stairs. He rounded the corner, stepped outside and jogged toward the entrance hall. Breathing deeply from exertion, he took in a familiar scent and stopped.

As he followed the aroma, he sensed it led past the tall iron fence. Pulling on the gate, he found it locked. Unable to stop himself, he scaled the iron barrier and landed on the other side. The sweet fragrance was intoxicating. Closing his eyes, he inhaled deeply, letting it fill his senses. He opened his eyes, looking around, and saw a small trail circle around the garden. He followed the path until he ended up in the center.

The path continued to encircle a huge granite and marble sculpture. It was beautiful. Atop the sculpture sat a large Pedalstem Lilly surrounded by small dancing stars. *That's weird. That sculpture isn't moving per say, but it feels alive.* The lily in fool bloom, large petals open and welcoming, and the stars seemed to radiate with pulsing cosmic energy. Awestruck by the sight, he felt a twinge of familiarity tugging softly at the back of his mind.

His chest swelled, his back straightened, he stood tall and felt proud just gazing upon it. Below the lily formed a small pool of water trickling down the front of the stone and into a small hot spring. Steam swirled into the air and mixed with the sweet aroma of flowers. *It's almost…magical.* Without realizing it, his feet had carried him close to the monument. His hand in the air, fingers close to brushing it, he heard a voice behind him and he froze. Turning his head and his body slowly, he saw Mr. Shauntsmiling.

"Beautiful, isn't it?"

"Yes it is."

The here and now finally washed over him and he dropped his hand. "Oh, Mr. Shaunt, I'm truly sorry, sir. I was on my way to see you when the garden caught my attention and I was uncontrollably drawn here. Sir, my deepest apologies. What is it that you would like me to do?"

"No need to worry, my boy. I figured that you needed your rest so I told the other stable hands they weren't to disturb you. Tomorrow, Kip and Kam are going to show you around, introduce you to the mounts, and give you the list of things that each one needs. They will also have a chore list they must complete by mid-day at which point, you will return to me. There will be errands that have to be run daily."

"Thank you. I do believe that I can handle that."

Chapter Six
Changes

Blaze stood next to Arabella, excited. "Are you ready for our daily walk around the castle?"

"Yes I am. You ready to lead the way this time, Blaze?"

"Yes! Finally. It has been weeks and I think I know this castle inside and out."

"Well, lead the way."

Giggling like a child, she grabbed Arabella by the arm and led her on their daily journey. She pointed out landmarks along the way. Stopping in the center of the room, she explained the layout of the banquet hall.

"Okay, so the door to the left by the stairs leads to the guest and maid quarters. The door behind the throne platform, of course, leads to my room. The door to the right leads to the kitchens and the main door in the center leads to the entrance hall."

"That's very good. Now, on to the hard stuff. This is easy. Show me what you have really learned."

"We'll get there. I want to be thorough."

Arm and arm, she walked the two of them through the door behind the thrones. Halfway down the hall, Arabella's question echoed off the walls.

"Where are we going from here?"

"Down past my bedchamber is Slaine's room. Around the corner is the stairs that lead to the top towers and upper quarters.

At the end of the hall is an archway that leads into the garden. Through the garden, if you follow the path to the very back, you will end up at a gate. The gate leads outside and you can go to the village from there."

"Very nice. I'm so proud of you, Blaze. I told you it would come back to you."

"Nothing came back to me. It's because I memorized it, although I have been getting flashes. Nothing I can make any sense of, though."

"What kind of flashes? What do you see?"

"Some of them go by too fast to really make out. Some are pictures of places or people. Do you know who Lady Red and Woody are?"

"Yes. They used to be the King and Queen of Pedalstem. Why do you ask?"

"I have been dreaming of them. They *used* to be King and Queen? What happened to them?"

"Yes, *used* to be. No one knows what happened. You dreamed of them? That is very interesting indeed."

"Why is that interesting?"

"Only but a few nowadays even remember them."

"Oh, I wonder why I dreamed of them, then."

"That's a very good question. One which I have no answer for."

That is strange. More puzzle pieces with no picture. Arm still hooked with Arabella's, she chatted about other small details as they walked under the arch and into the garden. *So, beautiful and peaceful. It always smells fresh and clean...new.*

"While we are here, can we go and look at that beautiful sculpture?"

"Whatever you want, dear."

Walking in the direction of the sculpture, she tried to explain how she felt when she got close to it. *Let's see if I can put this into words. I'm not sure if I understand it enough to explain it, but here goes.*

"It sounds crazy, but it feels as if it's calling to me. Come to think of it, when I first started getting flashes of things, I was standing by that sculpture. You think it means something?"

"How does it make you feel? Perhaps it's just because you are completely relaxed in the garden."

"I don't know. It feels like more than that, but my mind is bruised so it could be as you say. I'm just relaxed. This garden is very soothing."

Standing in front of the fountain, she stared at the Pedalstem Lilly in the center. Her body unwound and seemed to fill with energy at the same time. She felt stronger, empowered. Her mind clearing of confusion and doubt, she felt her heart beat faster and stronger as if filled with purpose.

"Can we sit and talk?"

"Yes. There is a bench right over there. You may talk to me anytime, Blaze, you know that."

Careful to keep to the path, she slowly walked the short distance to sit down. Once seated on the bench, she turned to Arabella and wondered where she should start.

"When I talk to you about my flashes and the possibility of my memories returning, you are always hopeful. When I speak of them to Slaine, or ask him a question about it, he gets agitated. He acts as if he doesn't want me to get well. Am I wrong for wanting to know what I know and not just rely on what he says?"

"No, dear. Perhaps he's just afraid you will remember something he doesn't want you to."

"Like what? I mean, what could be so bad that he would fear me remembering it?"

"Good question, but I can't give you an answer for it. I'm sorry. I suppose we will just have to wait until your memory returns."

"You know, Arabella, the answers you give sometimes have me thinking you know something. Are you withholding information and dropping clues, hoping that it might click something in my brain."

"What could be gained from that action, Blaze? I'm just an old woman. What do I know?"

She looks innocent sitting there with her shoulders shrugged and holding up her hands as if to say search me, *but I can't help but feel like she knows something. I just don't understand why she wouldn't tell me everything. Maybe she is afraid if she tells me it will interfere with my recovery. It's possible I guess, but still...*

"You know plenty and we both know it. Are you really telling me all you know?"

"Yes, dear. All I know, I have told you. How about we go back to the kitchen and make sure the food is being prepared? Lunch is only a few hours off."

"Sounds good to me."

Back on her feet, she hooked arms once more, walked out of the garden and headed for the kitchen. She still had one question that burned in her mind and she needed an answer so she could put it to rest.

"Arabella, how's Demarko?"

"He's fine, dear. He's working for Shaunt, helping in the stables and running castle errands. Why do you ask?"

"Um, no reason. I'm just worried about him. I haven't seem him around lately."

"Ah-huh! Well, Shaunt keeps him pretty busy."

"What?"

"Nothing, dear, nothing. Now, who isn't telling all she knows."

"Okay, fine. I see him a lot...well, his face anyway. Every time I get really happy or excited. He reminds me of that Woody fellow in my dreams. I think about him all the time. I was afraid to ask to see him since I'm trying my best to avoid Slaine. It's much easier to be around Demarko. Slaine is always so edgy. He has started to let his real colors show. He's getting rude and pops off with snide comments here and there. He really isn't a happy person. I often wonder why we married in the first place."

"Try not to worry too much, dear. I'm sure things will work out the way they're supposed to. Here, we're almost to the kitchen. Let's go in and make some tea. We can taste some of the food and aggravate the cooks about it."

"You think so?"

"What...aggravating the cooks? Of course I think so."

Her eyes took in the coy smile on Arabella's face. She smiled back and let the question go. *Okay, so she isn't going to elaborate on the question. I will let it go...for now.* Walking into the banquet hall seemed the same as entering a war zone. She watched in wide-eyed horror. People were running in all directions yelling, barking orders, and waving stacks of parchment in the air.

"Arabella, what's going on?"

"Oh, the time completely slipped my mind. This is normal for this time of year. It's preparations for the annual Fall Feast and weeklong festival. It's a huge event put on by you every year!"

"Is it fun? This looks to be a lot of work. When is it?"

"It's in about a month from now—"

"A month from now? Why are all of these people here now? Who *are* all of these people?"

"These are petitioners from far and wide along with messengers from other kingdoms requesting an invite to this year's celebration. Here, let's go over and sit down and I will explain it to you."

"This would be so much easier if my mind worked properly." She sat down at a nearby table.

"It's fine, dear. First off, all of the boys in brown pants and ruffled white shirts are the messengers. Shaunt will personally look over the requests and give an answer. Usually, that's what *you* do, but given your current state, he has decided to take that on. Mostly, he will just re-invite the people you approved of last year. The rest are vendors looking to score a sweet spot to sell their wares. As pronounced by your parents, all of Pedalstem attends as participants only. The festival's a celebration of the entire kingdom and its people from the royals all the way down to the smallest babe. The townsfolk even get to vote on who's invited this year as well as who is invited back. It's a grand affair and everyone has a great time. "

"Well, it sounds fun. I want to help. Just because my memories are gone doesn't mean I'm powerless. I'm glad that Shaunt is managing the guest list, but I can help with what is served as well as decorations. I'm getting excited just thinking about it."

"That would be great, Blaze. You and I usually do the decorating."

Clapping her hands softly and bouncing up and down, she tried unsuccessfully to contain her excitement. "Yeah! So, do we have a theme already? We do theme parties, yes? How long do we have exactly? Let's start drafting a plan so we can begin gathering supplies."

Quills scratching against parchment, soft whispers and the occasional *oh I like that* filled the room. Heads huddled together, she worked with Arabella on the plans for the feast. Her heart skipped a beat and her body jerked upright when she heard Slaine's voice behind her.

Hand on her chest, and catching her breath, she looked at him and spoke.

"Dear God, Slaine, you just about gave me a heart attack! Give me a little warning next time."

"What're you two all giggles about? I can hear you all the way down the hall."

"We're planning for the Fall Feast and Festival."

"Oh, fun," he said, rolling his eyes. "I just came to tell you, I'm going away for a while. It's castle business. I'll be back as soon as I can."

"Let me gather a few things and I will go with you. If it has to do with the Kingdom, I need to go."

"No! You're not going! You have this...this festival...thing, anyway. Lord knows I could care less about storytellers and rhyme thyme poets. Sometimes, there is good food, but this has always been *your* affair, not mine."

"Um, alright, I will see you when you return."

"Personally, I wish the whole affair to be cancelled. Depending on how my trip turns out, it just might be!"

She watched as he stomped out of the hall. Tightening her jaw and pressing her lips together, she held back the tears that threatened to turn loose at any moment. *Why does he always have to be such a spoilsport? Every time I get excited about something, he has to ruin it with his bad attitude. Why can't he just be nice?* The heat of anger coursed through her. Heart thumping hard in her chest and picking up pace, she felt her body tremble. Blaze took a deep breath, closed her eyes, and focused her mind before she asked Arabella a question.

"Why does he always have to trash my good mood? It's as if he stalks me, and the minute I'm smiling, he pounces."

Looking into Arabella's eyes, she saw her face soften and her eyes fill with sincere sorrow. Arabella's hand patted her own and she smiled at the gesture.

"I don't know, dear. Perhaps it's as you say…he's just not a happy person. Don't let it upset you. He's the only person in this entire kingdom who's not happy and looking forward to the celebration."

"You know, you're right. He'll just have to be unhappy all by himself. I just don't wear dark and dreary well."

"That a girl. How about we get back to work?"

Swallowing her anger and storing it for later, she refocused and concentrated on the festival.

"That's a great idea. Speaking of great ideas, I want to go down into the village and see the seamstress. I want everyone in town fitted for a new outfit for the festivities. The last few months have been hard on all of them, too. This will be my gift to them. I want to show them that even though I have been away and ill, I haven't forgotten them."

"I think they'll love that. I'll go and have Shaunt send for the seamstress."

"No. Don't have them come here. Send word that we will come to call tomorrow afternoon. Also, have Shaunt keep those men with the fancy fabrics and put them in the guest rooms for the night. I want them to accompany us tomorrow."

"Right away. What're you going to do while I'm gone?"

"I'm going to stay here and sift through some of the decorations we had the guards haul in."

"Sounds great. I'll see you around dinner time then."

Now, what do we have in these boxes? Knees on the floor, bent over a crate, she pulled out garlands and flowers and separated them into piles. Dirt and dust stuck to her sweaty skin as she continued to work through the fourth box. Using her arm, she wiped at her sweaty brow before getting off the floor. On her feet, she turned and saw Slaine standing by the table looking at her with a sour expression on his face.

"I thought you were leaving?"

"I am. I just figured I would come by and see if you have changed your mind about cancelling this blasted affair?"

I hate that smug look. "Why would I do that? The whole kingdom is buzzing about it."

"It nonsense, that's why."

"The whole town is looking forward to this along with all the children. Why take that happiness from them?"

"Why do you care, should be the real question. They mean nothing to us. We are the King and Queen. We tell them how it's to be, not the other way around."

So cold and heartless! Standing tall and straight, she folded her arms across her chest and glared at him. *If this is the way it is to be, so be it. I'm not backing down.*

"If you don't want to attend, then don't. You have made it obvious that you want no part of it. What do you want? I'm busy."

"First of all, how dare you speak to me that way."

Quicker than she thought, her eyes missed his movements and her body went spiraling into the hard floor. Crawling onto her hands and knees, she turned her head and glared at him as more bile fell from his mouth.

"I'm the King. I want you to cancel this ridiculous affair. I can think of better ways to waste our time. These people are not worth all this."

I won't bend to his will simply because he demands it. No amount of smacking me around is going to change how I feel about my people. I'll do what is needed to keep them happy and safe no matter what the costs.

"I'm *not* going to cancel! It will break their hearts. I refuse to sadden my people that way. With or without you, the festivities will continue. If not here, I will hold it in the village!"

"They aren't people in the sense that they're important. They're but dirt beneath our shoes and I demand that you stop spending time with them."

I'm done with this! "I hope you aren't too disappointed in that illusion you live in." She got on her feet squared her shoulders and stalked out of the room. *Let him be alone with his friends, disgust, and hateful. He can enjoy that party without me.*

Chapter Seven
Festive and Unfestive Festival

Sunshine on my face and wind in my hair, today is a great day to start the festival. Looking forward to the day's festivities, she walked over and joined Arabella and Shaunt.

"Are you two ready?"

"Yes, we're just waiting on you, My Lady."

"I think I want to go and taste some of that roasted quail first. It smells wonderful."

"That it does."

Following the aroma of cooked meat, she walked with Arabella and Shaunt in search of the quail vendor. Her face wore a bright smile, her body was calm, and her spirit soared with happiness. Blaze's mouth watered as she spotted the meat vendor just a few feet ahead. Approaching the counter, she felt her eyes go wide at all the different meats.

"What will you have, la—I mean what can I get you, My Lady?"

Well, he is a burly looking man. He has such a sincere smile. "I came over in search of your roasted quail, but now that I'm here, it all looks and smells great. I'm having a hard time deciding."

"Me, too," Arabella added.

"Then, there is only one choice to be made. How about I get you a little of all of it? A little sampler, perhaps?"

"That sounds great. One for each of my friends here, too."

"Yes, My Lady. Here you go."

Careful not to burn her hand, she grabbed the plate and took a bite of the roasted goodness. The meat fused together and melted on her tongue, and closing her eyes, she savored the taste. *Mmm this is the greatest! It tastes just as good as it smells.* Opening her eyes, she turned to the vendor.

"This is delightful! I would like to invite you to the feast. Arabella here, is a great cook as well. I would love to see what you think of *our* cooks…maybe give them some pointers."

"Now, hold on there. I make an excellent roasted quail. You just don't remember."

"Actually, truth be told, My Lady, that would be Arabella's recipe. I just tweaked it a bit. I added a pinch more garlic and basil."

Lips in a hard line, she tried to keep the smile from her face. "Oh, is that so. Well, perhaps you don't need to come to the feast. What do you think, Arabella?"

"Oh, stop, Blaze. You know well that I wouldn't keep anyone from the feast."

Wow, she fakes it well. She looks all mad with her eyebrows bunched together and pointing her finger at me, but I can see her mouth twitching. She is fighting hard not to smile. She clasped her hands together and watched the woman's finger bounce as she spoke, trying not to laugh.

"And I can see that smile you are trying to keep hidden, young lady. Why, if you were a few years younger, I would turn you over my knee for giving me such a hard time."

Blaze burst out laughing, then looked at the others. Shaunt laughed a bit, followed by the vendor, and of course unable to control it, Arabella joined in.

"I had forgotten how sensitive Arabella is about her cooking skills. You're lucky she didn't turn you over her knee anyway."

"Can it, old man. I'm not sensitive."

"Old man—"

"Arabella, it was your idea."

"What? When did I say? Oh, Blaze, how about while we were

out, you gave me a hard time? Hmm, I just don't remember that?"

"Well, you didn't use *those* words. You did say just last month we needed to aggravate the cooks about the food."

"Well, that's not what I meant."

"Well, you're the best cook, so I figured we should end with you." Holding her lips together tightly, she tried to wipe the smile from her face.

"Blaze, you'd better be careful. She might smack you with a wooden spoon or something."

"At this rate, probably a big skillet, but since you said I was the best, I'm going to let it slide this one time."

I knew she wouldn't be able to scorn me without laughing. "Alright, fine. I'm done now. Let's go see the rest of the festival."

"Well, that is the safest thing you have said in the last five minutes."

Blaze winked and smiled quickly at the quail vendor before turning and strolling away.

The heat from the plate warmed her left hand. In the other hand, she held the fork and worked at eating the food as they walked to enjoy the rest of the festival.

"Well, I think I need to get back to the castle. I don't think I can hold anymore. It has been a fun and eventful day."

"Yes, it has. I'm glad that you decided to hire the other seamstresses, It'll make the outfits come together much faster."

"And thank you for your help, Arabella."

"Personally, My Lady, I would give my life for you, but I think that if I have to hold one more roll of this fabric, my arms are going to fall off."

"I know, Shaunt, I'm sorry. I have rather gotten carried away today. I mean, look at this stuff. I have the seven rolls of fabric, jewels, chains, ropes, and all of this needlework the women of the village made me. I think my arms might fall off, too."

"Yes, I second that. Blaze, you made your people so happy today. They love visiting with you."

"I loved it. All the men and their stories, and battle scars, the woman giving me their needlework and recipes and the children with their antics and games. I have had so much fun. Between the food and play, I'm exhausted. Maybe tomorrow, we can see the mock battles and jousting competitions.

Rearranging her load, she continued to walk toward the castle. A few feet away, she heard Demarko call her name. Happy and surprised, she turned quickly to see him. *Oh, how I love the sound of his voice.*

"Demarko, how are you"

"Good, My Lady. Let me carry that for you. Oh, I almost forgot, these are for you."

She handed the fabric to Demarko in one hand and used the other to grab the flowers and put them to her face. Inhaling, she smelled the sweet aroma and smiled at Demarko.

"These are beautiful, Demarko, thank you. Pedalstem Lillies are my favorite. They remind me of the sculpture in the garden, only smaller."

"Ahem."

Why is Shaunt giving him that look? The one that implies they are up to something.

"How was the walk, Demarko? Did you find anything interesting?"

"Yes—"

"Well, hello, Demarko."

His voice sounded in her ears and immediately darkened her mood. He forcefully jerked the flowers from her hand and his face, smug and superior, glared at Demarko. *Slaine here to ruin the day.* Her hands cupped as if she still held the flowers. Her eyes narrowed and she watched helplessly as Slaine slammed the flowers into Demarko's chest. *How dare he? He may have given me a smile, but his mood is worse than ever.*

"Here, give these to some lass. Maybe she'll give you something in return."

Unable to move, her arms in his tight grip, his mouth closed over hers. Using all of her strength, she tried pushing him away. It was no use.

Having her space back, she pulled away and glared at him. *Ugh! What a brute.* With her arms, she wiped away his disgusting kiss and tried to calm herself. Slaine's eyes still glared at Demarko, so she stepped between them to get his attention. "You seem happy. Did all go as you planned?"

"Yes. I have missed you so."

Prepared for it this time, she turned her head at the last minute. Anger fueled the fire in her chest, her stomach churned, and she tightened her fist to keep her hands from shaking. She turned back and looked at him when he stepped away. *He's so arrogant. Why did I marry him? This had to be an arranged marriage. He's a giant ass!* Her wrist in his tight grip, he forced her to follow him as he dragged her away. At the last minute, she reached over, grabbed the flowers out of Demarko's hand and mouthed, *thank you.*

"I have someone for you to meet. I have finally found my brother."

Great. One of you isn't enough. Now, I have to put up with two? I was having such a nice day!

"Deklan has been gone for a long time, studying in his field. We crossed paths recently. He was leaving his master, Frankah. I received word a while back that he wished to return, due to her death. I believe she was more to him than just his teacher. I'm inclined to think he loved her. I'm so excited for you to meet him. I'm sure you will soon love him as much as I do."

I hope he has a better attitude than Slaine here. If not, my days have just gotten darker.

Two feet through the banquet hall doors and she froze. Her muscles refused to move. Her mind raced her heart and she broke out in a cold sweat. *I'm doomed. He is the embodiment of evil. Everything about him screams menace and mayhem.* Her body in shock, she could only stare.

Long, black robes covered his small frame, which contrasted with his milky white almost sickly skin tone. His tousled black hair barely passing his ears looked as dirty as the boots nearly hidden beneath his robe. Long, slender, gangly hands revealed liquid silver fingernails that matched the starburst ring on his finger. His eyes were just as menacing as his brother's. Sparkling silver pupils rimmed in the void of darkness. *Yes, he looks as if he has been pulled from the darkest void of hell and dropped into the world to wreak havoc on innocent souls.*

"Blaze, where are your manners? Aren't you going to say hello?"

"Hell...hello. I'm Blaze."

Chills ran up and down her spine when his cold skin engulfed her in a hug. *As cold as his skin is, I wouldn't be surprised to find out he is really dead. Ha! Dead. Now there's a horrible, yet comforting thought.* Moving her hands up and down on her arms, she attempted to put some warmth back into them. Her frame shook once with a final chill as her fear helped to warm her body.

"Her voice is as beautiful as the rest of her. You have done well, my brother. Are there any little Slaine's running around?"

That is a morbid thought. More Slaine's...over my rotting corpse!

"No, Deklan, we haven't any children, yet. Here, let's have a seat and catch up."

Three familiar voices and a commotion from behind her brought her out of her daze. Turning around, she saw Arabella, Shaunt, and Demarko enter the banquet hall. She stepped one foot toward the kitchen and found herself grabbed by the wrist yet again. His whispered words sent chills down her spine.

"No! You will join my brother and me. Sit!"

Her muscles were tight and stiff as she sat down. Blaze felt like a lamb among wolves. She was aware of sweaty palms, frenzied pulse and a hectic heart rate as she eyed the two men, awaiting her fate. Slaine's arrogant voice filled the hall.

"Arabella, bring a bottle of our finest wine and three goblets. Shaunt, go down and fetch some of that roasted quail. Oh, and Demarko, feel free to return to shoveling manure as that fits your station. My brother and I will be along to visit you."

I have to get out of here. I'm suffocating. "You know it's been a really long day. I think I'm going to retire to my room for the night. Deklan it was…uh…have a good night." *I should have known it wasn't going to be that easy. Must he always grab me?*

"No, you will stay. I have missed you, and Deklan would like to get to know you. Isn't that right, Deklan?"

Jerking her arm out of his grip, she stared at him for a moment, then sat down. "I don't like to be man-handled. Thank you!"

"She is a bit flippant don't you think, Brother? I'm not sure that I would put up with that kind of behavior from a woman."

Blaze drew air in her lungs preparing to fire back, but Arabella showed up, saving her from herself. Looking at Arabella as she filled the glasses, she noticed a funny expression. Eyebrows creased together, she gave a questioning look at the woman. Keeping her gaze on her friend, she watched the woman make her way around the table. Soon, Arabella's whispered warning found her ears as she filled the wine glass.

"Watch yourself around these two. Slaine is but a kitten compared to Deklan."

Blaze took a sip of her wine as she watched Arabella hustle back to the kitchen.

She couldn't, help it, but her eyes rolled and a snort escaped her at hearing Deklan say he wanted to continue his priesthood. *That's a wagon full of dung. 'Cause his appearance and demeanor scream saintly!*

"Did you say something, Blaze?"

"Oh, I'm sorry…had something stuck in my throat." *Yeah, I'm choking on the crap falling out of his mouth.*

Sipping more wine, she watched the brothers and their conversation. *Well, that didn't take long. At this rate, they are going to be through that bottle in less than an hour. That would be refill number three. They are well-lit and getting loud. Time for me to go.* Getting out of her chair and stretching her muscles, she prepared to hurry to her room.

"I think I'm going to go to bed now. I'm beat. Besides, I need to get these flowers in some water."

"Is something wrong with your wine?"

"No—what're you doing?"

She looked from Deklan to Slaine and her anger flared as her adrenaline rushed through her. She knew what he planned to do when he snatched the flowers from her hand, and she couldn't stop it. Her fingers itched and burned from the sudden jerk of the stems. Her gaze went from her hands, to his face, to the flowers. Petal by petal, leaf by leaf, she watched as he shredded the small bouquet. They fell piece by mutilated piece dying on the concrete floor.

"No! You'll sit down and stay here. I'll walk you to your room in a bit. As for these flowers, I gave them back for a reason."

Tears welled up and spilled over, but her head seemed light from the sudden rush of rage. She felt flush across her cheeks. Her hands balled into fists as she stood staring at him and the decimated flowers.

"I'm sorry, Blaze. Please forgive me. I have just missed you so. I had this grand vision of the three of us laughing, talking, and having a great time together. Please stay. Have one more glass of wine and then I'll walk you to your room. Promise."

"Fine." She dropped her body in the chair and reached for a glass. She found only air. "What?"

"I'm sorry. Here's your glass. I was refilling it for you."

She reached across the table and snatched her glass out of Deklan's hand. Blaze took a few cleansing breaths and attempted to control her emotions. Hand swiping across her cheeks, she removed the remains of painful tears. *Almost over. Might as well stay. I'm too mad to sleep now.* Glass in hand, she turned it up, downed its contents and slammed it flat on the table. She counted to three hundred very slowly. *That is about five minutes. I'm done.*

"My wine is gone! I'm going to my room now."

She shot up too quickly, and confusion took over when she flopped back into the chair. *What's going on? Wine can't affect you that quickly. Ohhh!* A hand on each side of her head, she tried to keep it from spinning. *Something's wrong.* Slaine's voice penetrated her ear.

"Blaze, are you all right? Why did you down it so fast?"

"Wha...what did you do?"

"This isn't my fault. You downed the wine. I should have

warned you, but I didn't think you would've done that."

"Warned me about what?"

"You are a light weight when it comes to wine."

Head slamming onto the table, she tried to will it to move, but nothing happened. *Why can't I move? My body feels like heavy rubber.*

"Deklan, I need to get my bride to her room before she hurts herself."

Head bobbing back and forth, arms dangling, she lay limply in his arms. Her body jarred around with his quick movements as he seemed to rush out of the banquet hall. Tapestries and light blurred in her vision as he swept them away down the hall toward her room. Using all her strength and anger, she worked at controlling her own body. *This is very bad. I have to push through this. This isn't right.*

Gaining some control, she clumsily slapped her hand onto the side of Slaine's, head. *Yes! Anger is the key. It must be burning through the alcohol. He didn't even move. I'll have to try something else.* Head still dizzy, she pulled it up and rested it on his shoulder. *One...two...three!* Her elbow in his ribs and a hand on his chest, she shoved herself out of his hold, but her body slammed into the concrete floor. *Ouch, should have thought that through.* She rolled onto her hands and knees working to get off the floor. Her arms trembled from trying to support her weight.

"No, get your hands off me." Leaning on one hand, she batted his hands away with the other.

"Stop that. Let me help you. How do you expect to walk when you can barely hold your own head up. Put your arm around my shoulder. I will help you walk, at least."

The brutal truth of his words slammed into her and she swung her arm around his shoulder and let him help.

Feet missing steps and half dragging, she was surprised to see how much progress they made.

"Can you stand on your own? I need to open the door."

Reaching her hand out, she flipped the latch and opened the door. "It's not hard."

Toes scraping the ground, she watched the bed move closer as he carried her into the room.

"Bed."

Oh! Her frame bounced when he dropped her onto the mattress. *Soft...sleep...finally.* Her body almost numb, mind falling into a fog, she was faintly aware of his hands on her legs and ankles.

What...hands doing...move. Lifting her head, her eyes squinted and she saw him taking off her shoes.

"It's fine, just go." Her head flopped back onto the pillows when his hands dropped from her skin. Her eyes closed and blackness appeared.

She blinked her eyes and looked around in confusion when she felt her body pressed against his chest and shoulders. The sound of her zipper unzipping, pulled her from the fog. Pushing away and still uncoordinated, she fell onto the floor. Her arms held her body half off the ground. She turned her eyes and looked at him.

"I'll do it. Just go to your room or something. I'm fine."

"Nonsense. You can hardly hold yourself up. Look...you're teetering back and forth. You're going to drop at any moment. Let me help you into bed and then I'll leave."

She felt the warmth from his hands when he lifted her from the floor and placed her back on the bed. Head on soft pillows and flat on her back, she felt him slide off her dress. *No, no, no!* Her mind protested, but her body wouldn't move. She lay half-unconscious and unable to stop it. *He stopped. Maybe he will leave as he said he would.* His voice sounded as soft as velvet when he whispered in her ear.

"I'm going to build a fire so that you don't catch a chill when the wine wears off."

Her body still and unmoving, her mind drifted into a blank state and she fell into the cloud of sleep...

She felt the steam from the hot spring combined with the heat of their bodies touching one another. Her neck laced with wet kisses, his hands left an electric pulsing current along the curves of her body, touching, caressing. Low soft moans filled the air. Arching her back and repositioning herself, she ached for the feel she was craving. Warm air filled her senses and tickled her skin where he touched her. Pulling his face to her, she kissed him hard tasting his sweet breath mixed with hers. *Too sweet, like wine.* She tried pushing him away. His touch became more forced and painful. Her wonderful dream turned into a nightmare.

Once her eyes opened, it revealed what she feared. *Slaine.* His mouth was on her chest and his moan vibrated her skin. Pulling her anger forward, giving her strength, she shoved him off. She snatched at the blanket, clutching them to her chest and screamed at him.

"Get off me!"

Breathing heavily, she tried to remember what happened.

"What is wrong with you? It's me, your husband Slaine."

She watched his movements as he got off the floor and towered over her, yelling back. Anger still flowed through her, she thought about what he said and tried to make sense of it. *Husband? Slaine? What happened? Wine...drunk...passed out...hot spring...soul mate...husband Slaine. Huh? Why doesn't this fit? What's wrong?* Her mind catching up had her body filling with rage. It started at her toes and by the time it reached her face, she could hold her tongue no more.

"How dare you! Is this why you wanted me to have that wine? What exactly was in my glass? Do not insult my intelligence by saying just wine. Did you think since I wouldn't go to you, willingly your next move should be to get me drunk and take it? Get out now! I don't even want to look upon your disgusting face."

"What exactly are you talking about? I did nothing wrong I'm your husband! That's my right! It's your duty to me *as* my wife!"

Still wound tight in rage, all she could do was stare as she watched him yell and point a finger at her. Her eyes on the pacing beast, she was surprised when he opened his mouth to speak. His voice had softened.

"I am sorry. It's just...I lay down next to you...I miss you so much. I just thought the wine might take the edge off. I figured it would all come back to you if I lay with you in that way. I thought it was working. What happened? You were responding."

How do I explain this? I can't tell him I was dreaming and I'm not certain he was the man in it. I am horrible, I know, but I can't change my heart at will. Or because he demands it. Man in my dreams or not, I will not sleep with him. I'm not in love with him. Tears in her eyes dripping from her cheeks, she stared at him. His shoulders sagged. He hung his head in shame and one small tear rolled down his cheek. She tried to describe how she felt.

"Please understand. I don't really know you. Well, I don't remember you. You're like a stranger to me. I'm sorry this hurts you. I'm not doing this out of spite. Where is my nightdress? We can talk some more once I'm dressed. That would help me feel better."

Caught in his gaze, she watched his demeanor change. His body stiffened, his hands curled into fists and the fire in his eyes flamed up and danced with rage. Movement. He bent over, picked up her nightdress, and threw it at her.

"Here is your nightdress. Put it on!"

The sound of pants swishing together as he stormed from the room followed by the slamming of the wooden door, filled her ears when he left. Silence for only a second. Quickly sliding into her nightdress, she jumped up, ran to the door, and locked it. Her frame against the door, she breathed heavily and listened to his footsteps stomp away. Fear gone and anger leaving her body, she felt the weight of emotions take over. *I just don't feel anything for him. Well, right now, I feel plenty for him, just not what he wants me to feel. I don't know how to fix this. I can't force my heart to do what I want. I wish my memories weren't gone because this wouldn't be a problem. I would know my husband.* Tears ran down her face as her cries came to life. Climbing back into bed, she pulled the cover over her head and gave into her fitful sobs.

Her breathing evened out and her tears stopped as her fit neared its end. *I will have to try harder, I guess. Maybe if I spent more time with him, I could get to know him better. Perhaps I could get comfortable enough to meet his needs, at least until my true feelings for him return.* Feeling peaceful about it, she cuddled under the blankets and fell asleep watching the couple once more…

Keeping with his stride, she wrapped her arm around his waist and walked toward the carver's station. Something glimmered in the corner of her eye catching her attention. Turning her head in the direction of the shiny objects, she noticed a jewel vendor. Red maneuvered toward the vendor, feeling Woody change his direction and follow her.

"Oh, those are pretty."

"Well, hello, My Lady."

"Hello. Can I see that Emerald neckband, please?"

"Of course. Here, you go. Oh, Mr. Woody, I'm glad that you have arrived. Here is the Topaz ring your father asked for. Keep it safe."

She heard Woody's voice in her ear and turned his direction in time to see the vendor hand him the ring. Did he just wink at Woody? Maybe I'm seeing things. I really need to get some sleep tonight.

"That's really pretty, Woody. Your father has good taste. I bet your mother will love it."

"I will pass that along. Um, can I borrow your finger for a moment? Your hands are the same size as my mother's…Father wants me to be sure it will fit properly."

"Of course." Lifting her arm, she held her hand up, her ring finger raised slightly higher than the rest and waited for Woody to slip on the ring. Her hand shook slightly as the cool gold circle slid down her finger and rested there. How many times I have dreamed of this? Him sliding a ring on my finger. It's almost a dream come true. Only he isn't asking me to marry him, rather, he is testing a fit for his mother. An errand for his father. *Staring at the ring, she noticed the light from the sun bounce off the stone sending glimmering sparkles onto everything. She looked from the ring on her finger to Woody's face.*

"Woody, this stone is the exact color of your eyes."

"Really? Huh. How about I put this away for now. I don't want

to lose it."

She took a deep breath, calming her emotions and watched the ring slide off her finger and drop into a small leather pouch. Well, it was nice while it lasted. One day… *Eyes glazed over deep in thought, she hadn't paid attention to the conversation until the word Emerald filled her ears. Looking over in Woody's direction, she saw him pull the leather strings, shut his pouch, and smile at her.*

"How about some Pumpkin spiced tea?"

"Sounds great. It's a little frigid."

She slipped her right arm through his, placed her other hand on his inside shoulder and leaned in close as they walked. Once at the tea vendors, she grabbed a glass filled with the liquid.

"Do you want to sit on that hay bale?"

"Sure."

Bending in half, she sat on the hay bale with his arms around her. Hard pieces of straw poked her legs, but she didn't care. This is nice. Cool night air and his warm body next to me. Oh, Lord! *Nodding in the direction of the two youths clearly headed in their direction, she hoped it would end better than it had last time.*

"Here come our new friends."

"Want to try and make a run for it…pretend we don't see them?"

"No, they would probably just follow us. Better to just stay and get it over with. I hoped maybe it would be better than last year, but they don't look happy…so I'm guessing not."

Head huddled close to Woody's, talking softly, she felt their presence before their shadows darkened her vision. Her eyes on the skinny boy Slim, she watched his smug smile fill his face and his chest take in air right before he spoke. He looks like a blowfish.

"What's this? Haven't you tired of this insignificant boy, yet? You should not dress down your beauty by hanging with boys. You need a real man."

She felt Woody's muscles tense and prepare to move. She touched his arm and let him know to wait.

"You are right, Slim. I do need a real man. I have a great idea. Why don't you and your sidekick run out and fetch me one. Oh, but wait, there's one right here. He's sitting right next to me. Thanks a heap, boys. I wouldn't have been able to do that without you. Now that you have saved the day, why don't you run along now?"

Watching from the corner of her eye, she saw Woody drop his head, close his eyes, and take a deep breath. She felt his body tense and flex with every word she spoke. She turned her head and her attention to Woody to check on him and heard D start to say something. Her attention moved to the boy.

"You pampered little priss. How dare you speak to my brother that way. You shall pay dearly for that."

It happened in slow motion. She looked from Slim to D. She felt Woody rise at the same time as D's hand. Woody stepped in front of her, then D and Slim flew through the air, landing a few feet away, flat on their backs. Peeking around Woody's frame, she saw the boys cussing and getting up from the ground. Uh oh. Her eyes glued to the scene and her heart in her throat, she didn't know how this would play out. Her father walked over and helped the boys from the ground.

"What is going on here?"

"Thank God you arrived, King Alexander. My brother D and I were just talking to the princess and this jealous oaf pushed us. We did nothing to warrant his attack."

"Is that true, D?"

"Yes. I think he should be flogged...publicly."

She couldn't believe her ears when their answers passed their lips. Liars! Her face heated and her pulse raced as she watched the exchange of lies.

"Run along. I will come and speak to your parents in a while."

Her mouth gaped open, her body heat rose higher. She couldn't believe her father would believe those boys. She jumped to her feet and tried to push Woody out of the way to get to her father. She ran into Woody, stone still, blocking her way and keeping her behind him.

"Wait! I want to make sure they leave."

She stepped around Woody and watched the boys leave in one direction while her father walked toward her. Her nerve gone, she stared at her father's towering frame and swallowed hard, feeling as if she needed to apologize for something.

"My Lord, I assure you, I acted in Red's best interest. I wasn't acting like some jealous animal. The older boy, D, raised his hand to swing at her and I moved instinctively to protect her."

Feet stuck in place, she looked from her father to Woody as the King closed the distance between them. A huge gust of wind left her lungs and her body relaxed when she saw her father smile and put his hand on Woody's shoulder.

"I know, Son. I saw the whole thing. I'll be speaking to their parents in a few minutes, but not for what they assume. I have been hearing a lot about them lately. I'm glad to know that my instincts about you were right. I told you last year, the first time I let you take her out of my sight, I knew she would be safe with you, and just now, you have proved it."

"Thank you, King Alexander. Your trust in me means a lot, especially when it comes to Red"

"Any time, Son."

"Father, why did you act as if you believed them?"

"It makes what is going to happen later, much easier."

"Makes what easier?"

"By now, they know they are in deep trouble. What you, or they, didn't see is a small group of undercover guards. I told them to wait until they get a few feet away, to ensure they think they got away with it, then snatch them and have the boys and their parents waiting for me. No one, and I mean no one, will raise a hand in anger toward my princess or anyone else. This is a peaceful town and I aim to keep it that way. However, I'm a bit biased. Had Woody been to slow to stop that boy...let's just say that D kid would be missing the hand he struck you with."

"Wait, Father..."

"I love you, sweetheart. I have to go."

Mouth open to question him, she slowly shut it when he turned and walked away. "I will just ask him about it later. He left so soon because he saw that I had put two and two together. And it definitely added up to four."

"What are you talking about, Red?"

"Four! Small group of guards? My father has four elite groups of guards, spies and such, and there are four in each group."

"I love you, but I still don't understand what you are talking about."

"Think about it. How did he see what was going on? Why was he so close when it happened? I will tell you how and why. He sent his guards to spy on us, and knowing my father, he gave them certain orders. Remember, we told him about those two before. I'm sure when the guards saw those two head back this way, they sent for him. He would be close."

"Um, love? Why are you mad? We did nothing wrong."

"I know. I'm mad because he sent guards to watch over us like we are babies or something."

"I didn't see them yesterday. Perhaps he just sent them today. You heard what he said...he has been hearing a bunch of stuff about them. Maybe...I think he sent the guards to watch them, not us. He didn't say what he heard...just that he heard it."

"I don't know..."

"Stop pouting. He loves you and wants to protect you."

She felt warmth on her back where his hand rested, pulling her close to him. Placing a smile across her face, she leaned her head on his chest, and shivers went down her spine when he whispered in her ear.

"Would it make you feel better if I told you I had a surprise for you and we could ditch the guards in the process?"

"Yes. I like surprises and getting to ditch the guards, well, I love that idea at the moment."

"Follow me."

Her hand in his, he led her past the festival and soon they disappeared beyond the tree line. Turning her head from left to right, looking at everything, she took in all the vibrant colors and shades. Captivated by what she saw, she had to blink to be sure she really was seeing it. The setting sun cast a red-orange haze *peeking through the trees. It seemed to reach the sky itself and flow straight down to the soft lush green grass. Flowers colored by the rainbow, blades of green swayed in the cool breeze, and animals played in the brush.*

"Wow, this is wonderful. I have never been beyond the tree line and into the woods before."

"I'm glad you like it, but this isn't what I want to show you."

Hand still locked into his, she walked on, and they talked of the different trees and flowers. The sun slowly departed the sky. Her eyes covered, he led her like a blind man for a few more feet. Clumsily, her feet moved forward, hands gripping his shoulder for support. She bumped into his body when he unexpectedly stopped.

"Why did we stop?"

"Because we're here. Keep your eyes closed. I'm going to remove my hands. I'll tell you when to open them."

"I have them closed." She felt the heat leave her skin when he removed his hands. With a smile on her face, her heart building momentum and hands clasped together, she waited to hear his voice.

"Now, you can open them."

She opened her eyes and looked around. It left her breathless and almost speechless. So much color. Tall trees encircled them resembling a protecting battalion of guards. Branches, reddish-brown in color, sprouted big dark leaves stretching out as if to mimic arms keeping them hidden from the world. A cottage perched in the background, small and simple. Blades of green covered the forest floor as if a soft carpet. Flowers vibrant and bursting with color dotted the area similar to splotches of paint on plain canvas.

Head slowly turning, taking it all in, she had never seen anything so beautiful. Small rays from the sun peeked through the trees while steam, mixed with honeysuckle, filled her senses. She noticed the hot spring sitting in the center surrounded by small gray and silver stones. Steam floated toward the sky, the water was calm and inviting, and in the back corner of the circle was a small patch of Pedalstem Lillies.

"Red? Do you like it?"

Mind and body overwhelmed with the rainbow of color and raw beauty, she could only shake her head yes in response. She felt his hands on her back and stomach and his chest on her side so she turned to him.

"It is beautiful. When did you do this?"

"As much as I would like to take credit for it, almost all of it was already done. I just cleared away the debris and planted some of the Pedalstem Lillies. Oh, and I placed the stones around the spring so it looked like the one in garden."

His hand on her chin and locked in his beautiful stare, she watched his lips move as he spoke.

"I hope that we can enjoy this place together alone someday. It can be our little hideaway. It's a bit far from the castle. If you won't feel comfortable here, I would understand."

"No, it's wonderful. I love it here already."

Bodies nestled on the grass, she leaned into him and just watched the flowers move in the breeze, the steam float into the air and she felt perfectly content. They sat huddled in each other's arms enjoying the sensation their touch brought to the skin and listened to the love song in their, hearts and ears.

"How did you find this place?"

"Well, after I left your room last night, I was too awake to sleep. Therefore, I decided to go for a walk. I just grabbed the lamp and left."

"Did your parents know?"

"No, it's different with boys than with girls, I suppose. Once they see me go to my room, they assume I stay there. Besides, boys are better at taking care of themselves. I was just wandering and found myself here. I knew it was perfect."

'When did you have time to get all of this done? I saw you this morning at breakfast?"

"I didn't leave here until this morning. When I came into the banquet hall, I had only been back long enough to wash and change clothes."

"So, you have not been to sleep yet?"

"No."

"Do we need to go back? If you need to sleep, I would greatly understand. We could always come back tonight."

"Red, I'm too happy to sleep right now. The look on your face when you opened your eyes was worth going without sleep. Although, there is one problem, now."

"What's that?"

"This was supposed to be a surprise for your birthday. Now, I will have to do something else."

"You have a few months."

"Actually, Red, it's six months, fifteen days, and some odd hours. At that point, we will both be the same age of eighteen. Well, for a little while, anyway."

Pushing him onto his back, hands on his chest, she leaned down and kissed him. She pulled away when she felt his hands on her lower back, and rested her head on his chest. Her eyes closed and her breathing even, she listened to his heart beat against his chest. This is perfect!

Chapter Eight
Decisions, Decisions

Out of a peaceful sleep, her eyes popped open and she knew what she needed to do. Excited about her resolution, Blaze threw the blankets off, got out of bed, and pulled on her robe. In a rush to be off, she grabbed the oil lamp next to her and headed out to find Slaine. Head bobbing from left to right, she checked the hall before venturing out. *I hope he's not still angry.*

Robe trailing behind, her feet padded across the cold concrete as she walked briskly to his room. Oil lamp in hand and the other holding her robe closed, she inhaled once, steadying her nerves. Hand fisted and reaching for the door, she stopped. *What's the right course of action here? Should I knock, or just walk in? I will just knock in case he is sleeping.* Small stabs of pain caressed her hand as her knuckles rapped on the wooden frame. Ears perked up and listening intently, she heard his footsteps on the floor. Air blew her hair back sending what felt like spiders dancing up her spine as he opened the door.

"Blaze, are you all right?"

He seems calm. She took a relaxing breath. "May I come in?"

"Yes."

She walked past him when he moved out of the way and closed the door behind her. Turning back to face him, she was engulfed in a warm hug. His lips were warm, she noticed, feeling his kiss on her head leaning into him for a moment before pulling away.

"I'm sorry I blew up at you earlier."

"I deserved it. I was wrong and I know it. You had every right and you *were* right. I should have been patient. I'm sorry, Blaze. I'll never do that again."

"This is a bad situation for everybody. You were wrong for what you did, but I do understand it. I don't know where to go from here, or how to fix it."

"Are you really tired? Would you care to go for a walk in the garden? I know you love it there."

"That would be nice, and yes, I love it there."

"May I hold your hand as we walk? If it's too much, I do understand."

Interlocking his hand with hers, he said, "No, that's fine."

"Shall we?"

"Yes." She followed him out the door and toward the garden.

Lavender, vanilla, and honeysuckle filled her senses as she entered the garden. Torches lit the walking path, birds chirped, and the stars shone brightly in the dark sky. Eyeing the sculpture took her breath away, leaving her speechless. The lily and stars seemed to pulse and glow with life and energy. She marveled at the sensation, the steam mixed with the cool air left on her skin, caressing and welcoming at the same time.

"Would you like to join me in the spring? It's kind of cool out here and well…it looks so inviting."

"Would I? I mean if it's all right with you. I don't want to push you."

"I'm fine with sitting next to you in the spring and enjoying the night air."

"That's all right with me. I promise to be a perfect gentleman. Would you like to change first, or just go in our birthday suits?"

"I'll just change when I get back to my room. My nightdress is fine. You could drop down to your skivvies if you want."

Letting the silk fall from her skin, she stepped into the warm water and sat down. As she glanced at Slaine, she had a hard time not laughing aloud. He floundered around as if a small child about to go for a swim on a hot day. His clothes flew off in all directions and were strewn across the grass due to ripping them off so fast. Water lightly splashed her face as he hurriedly walked past and sat down next to her. Her back on his chest, she felt his muscles relax as he breathed softly in her ear. *This is somewhat nice. Peaceful.*

"What do you want to talk about? Do you feel like talking?"

She moved into him when his arm reached around her and pulled her closer, answering her question.

"I love you. How about we just sit here for a while and see how that goes. Before you object, I'm not expecting anything. I just want to be near you without all the tension. This will be enough for now. I was just impatient before. I want you to know, I'm not mad at you, but rather, I'm furious with myself."

"I know. We'll work through this and it'll be better."

Inhaling the aroma of the garden and feeling his body relaxed, she closed her eyes and enjoyed the moment. Wrapped in his embrace, feeling his chest on her back, she let her mind wander to happier thoughts. *Demarko, once again. I always picture his face…and the rest of him. Focus on how am I to fix this thing with Slaine? We need to find some kind of compromise. What if he doesn't stop the next time? Perhaps I can meet somewhere near middle ground without having to go all the way.* She snapped back into reality when his whispered words floated into her ear.

"I hate to ruin this, but you are half asleep. You need to rest. It'll be light soon."

"Has it been that long already?"

"It has been quite a while, probably an hour, or so, at least. I will walk you to your room and make sure the fire is still going before I go to bed."

The nip in the air chilled her wet skin as she got out of the spring and reached for her robe. Silk garment in hand, she let him help her. Clothes wet and half frozen, she leaned into the warmth from his body as they walked back to her room. *This is nice, but feels awkward at the same time. My mind is telling me to say* this is your husband, *but my heart says different and wrong. Whatever happened messed up my heart and my mind. I wish I could just be better already. This is so frustrating not knowing. Perhaps Arabella was wrong. Following my heart will lead me away—not help me get closer. I have to make this work somehow.*

Her mind in many directions consuming her attention, she didn't notice they had stopped until he nudged her.

"Blaze, we're here. Are you okay? Why are you crying?"

She rolled her eyes and looked in his face as she tried to explain it. "It's nothing. I'm just tired, frustrated, and ready for my memories to come back. I'm trying."

"Don't let that upset you. Everything is as it should be. You're alive and well, and we're together. That's all that matters."

Sighing, she nodded her agreement. "Can we go in? It's very cold in this hallway."

"Yes. You are right, it is a bit chilly."

Blaze rushed through the door and immediately deviated to her chamber room to put on something dry and warm. "I will be right back. This nightdress is freezing me."

"I'm going to get a fire going…shouldn't take long to warm the room."

His muffled words reached her in the bathing room, but she was busy pulling off her wet clothes to pay much attention. Peeling off the sodden gown, she dropped it to the floor and goose bumps dotted her skin. Her body shuttered causing her movements to be quicker.

Sliding into the dry nightdress covered her body, but did nothing for the chill. Picking her wet clothes from the floor, she draped them over the tub as quickly as possible. She snatched a dry robe off the hanger and hurriedly put it on in attempt to warm herself. Her skin was not creamy white, but a soft pale blue. *Whew I need to stand by the fire. My teeth are chattering.*

Once back in the room, she could feel a wave of heat from the fire. Blaze stared at his body bent over the hearth. She paused and her mind flashed an image mirroring that same scene except one part. *Demarko?* Shaking her head slightly and looking again, it was Slaine bent over working the flames. *What happened? I swear that was Demarko standing there. Why do I have a memory of him building a fire in my room? Has he been in here before?*

"Nice and toasty! You will be throwing the blankets off in no time."

She blinked her room back into focus, strode over to the bed, and pulled the covers back. Body half under the covers, she noticed Slaine on his way out the door.

"Where are you going?"

"I'm going to my room as promised. The fire is going. It will stay warm enough while you sleep."

"Would you like to stay? Sleep is all I'm asking for, but I think I could handle that. If you want to, that is."

"I would love that. Are you sure about this?"

"Yes, I am. Besides, if I get uncomfortable, or you try anything funny, I will just push you off into the floor."

"Fair enough."

Holding the blankets to her chest, Blaze asked, "Can I ask you something?"

"Yes. You can ask anything you want."

"Is this the room we shared, or is it where I found you earlier?"

"It's this room. I have been sleeping in my study since your return. I didn't want to interrupt you getting better."

She watched as he ambled across the room toward the bed. His body looked relaxed. His shoulders seemed less tense and a smile so big, it actually reached his eyes. *Wow, he almost looks charming when he smiles that way.* She noticed him stop and give her a puzzling look.

"Um, Blaze? I don't want to offend you, or for you to think I'm trying anything, but my pants and clothes are now wet. Therefore, I have a few choices here. I can run to my room and change, I can sleep in wet clothes, or I can strip them off and sleep in the nude. Which would you prefer?"

"So long as you promise to behave yourself, I guess you can sleep naked, or you can run and change. However, if you decide to run and—"

"Stop right there. I prefer to sleep without the restriction of clothes, so if you're not going to thrash me…I will just drop my clothes and climb in."

"If that's what you prefer."

Reaching over with her finger and thumb, she turned the dial and snuffed the light. Sliding her frame down into the bed, she rolled onto her side and got comfortable. A small waft of air ran down her skin when he lifted the coverlet and snuggled close.

His body is warm and his touch is gentle, but still, something is off. Maybe it is just me. It must feel wrong simply because I don't remember him. That has to be it. What else could it be? What else would make sense? That's it. I know how to fix this.

Smile on her face and excitement coursing in her veins, she turned over slightly to speak to Slaine. She found him fast asleep with a wide grin on his face. *I wish I could be that content right now. Suppose I will tell him in the morning.* She pulled the blanket up to her ears, and head, sinking into the soft pillow, closed her eyes hoping for sleep. Drifting along the clouds of dreamland her nightly soap opera played again…

Two strides past the archway into the garden, Red stopped and her breath caught in her chest as she took in the scene. Something new. *Next to the sculpture stood a small round table draped in white linen, with two small candles on each side of a glass vase filled with white and red roses. The soft glow of the candlelight caressed the tips of each petal and mixed with the lavender sprigs covering the center. Two wooden chairs sat on either side. The garden and the table both looked very romantic. Before she could open her mouth to speak, he beat her to it.*

"I asked if we could have dinner out here just the two of us. If it's cold, we can go back into the entrance hall."

Staring at the small intimate setting, she felt a tear run down her cheek. Her body seemed to float above the clouds and her accelerated heart pounded in her ears keeping her firmly on the ground. Is this to be the moment I have been waiting for? How can I tell him the words, like and love are not enough in trying to describe how I feel at this moment.

Using the fingertips of her left hand, she wiped her tears away and looked into his bright, smiling face. His expression seemed mixed between confusion and fear. Smoothing the lines on his face with her hand, she looked into his eyes and smiled.

"I love it."

"Why the tears? If this isn't what you want, it won't hurt my feelings to go back inside the castle. I don't want—"

Leaning on her toes, she kissed him to stop him from speaking. Pulling away, her heels flat on the ground, she looked at him. The light reflected back in his eyes from his smile, heat and electricity building a fire.

"I'm sorry to have given you the wrong impression. I'm happier than I can explain. This is what I have wanted for a while now...just the two of us. People usually surround us. This is perfect."

"I'm glad. I feel the same way. I thought it would be nice to have some alone time. I meant what I said. If it gets too cold, let me know. We can always go back in."

"Nonsense. If I get chilly, we can just go huddle in that hot spring over there. I'm not giving up this moment for inconvenient cold weather."

"Well, since you put it that way, let me help you to your seat. Arabella will be arriving shortly with our meal. Before you ask, no, it's not what she's serving everyone else. I had her make something...different. I hope you approve."

Flattening her dress beneath her, she sat in the chair as he pushed it closer to the table. I could watch him walk all day and never get tired. The way his clothes move and stretch with each movement, proud, confident, and graceful. *In one swift motion, he sat down and when his hands returned to sight they, held a single Pedalstem Lilly. Wide, in full bloom, the petals blossomed open relative to an open and welcoming hand. The small veins running through each white petal in soft red lines pulsed with life. The stem was long, straight, and strong.*

"Happy eighteenth birthday, My Lady Red."

"*Thank you. How did you know that Pedalstem Lillies are my favorite?*"

"*You seem to favor them over all others I noticed, and of course you told me.*"

"*And what about the lavender? How did you know about the lavender?*"

"*You like those, too? I have to confess, I didn't know about that. I crumpled the lavender petals because you always smell that way to me. I know it's odd. It just reminds me of you.*"

"*Woody, it's not odd. I always add fresh lavender to my bath water because I love the aroma.*" Why am I blushing? It's not as if I don't know him well enough, or even intimately. We have come close to going all the way several times. Oh, thank God it's Arabella.

Eyes bright and full of happiness, she looked at her friend, Arabella, and returned her smile. She and her staff walked into the room with full hands. The woman placed two hot steaming plates in front of each of them followed by Maize, filling goblets with wine. Mouth open ready to say something, she closed it quickly when her friend shot her another quick smile and left. Staring at the empty archway, she heard Woody's voice fill her ears and she found at that moment that she didn't care why her friend hadn't spoken to her.

"*I remembered how much you liked the roasted quail at the festival, so I asked Arabella if she would make some for us.*"

"*It's wonderful. Thank you. It smells delicious. I can't believe you remembered.*"

"*It was our first date. That day put a smile on my face and a mark on my heart that will never fade.*"

"*I know how you feel. It was that same day and by the end of it, I knew I was in love with you.*" *Returning his smile, she looked down at her plate and ate the food, he had requested.*

Plate half-empty, fork in hand, she picked at her cheesecake while she talked. Leaning back in her chair and setting her fork on her plate, she watched as Arabella filled their glasses with wine. It was her third trip into the garden and she quickly disappeared once more. She watched the woman hustle out of the garden quickly and turned her attention back to Woody.

"Would you like to go for a walk?"

Placing her napkin on her plate, she scooted the chair back and took his hand. "Sure, where to?"

"Let's just see where we end up?"

Red soaked in the warmth of his body when she felt his arm around her waist holding her close. Heaven. He's like my own little walking fireplace stacked in a sexy human figure just for my pleasure. *Concentrating on the small talk and his face as they walked, she hadn't noticed they were beyond the tree line.* I should have known. This is where we always go, our little hideaway.

Cozy and warm, she snuggled close and tried to ignore the blades of grass tickling her thighs as they sat upon the ground. Head tilted toward the heavens, she watched the light leave the sky and stars float into sight, bright and beautiful. Her back vibrated as he spoke, his soft voice in her ears.

"I want to show you something, but I need you to lie down first."

Leaning forward and turning to face him, she wore a shocked look and crossed her body in mock horror. "Why, Woody what kind of girl do you think I am?"

Watching his reaction, she smiled inwardly. He rolled his eyes, but the smile never left his face and the light in his eyes only got brighter as he spoke.

"You are the right kind of girl, actually."

Her back lay on the soft grass, her hands in his hair, her lips moved with his, kissing him. Heat filled her body despite the coolness of the air playing against her skin. Breathing heavily, hands on his shoulders, she stared in his eyes when he pulled away. The fire in his eyes matched the heat of his body. Pure bliss!

"Now, stay still and keep your eyes closed until I tell you to open them."

"Alright, fine."

Closing her eyes, she took a deep breath. Chills popping up as daisies in a field ran along her skin when the heat from his hands moved away from her. Confusion crossed her face, but her eyes stayed closed when a soft buzzing sound filled her ears. What is that sound?

"You can open them now."

Feeling his warm hand on her stomach, she opened her eyes, and the sight before her astounded her. The sky was a deep dark blue, almost black, stars bright and shining, and yet, in front of her were not stars, but just as beautiful. Small sparks of light blinked against the night sky, never lighting the same place twice, but just as bright as any star.

"It's beautiful. How did you do that?"

"I'm not sure. I was out here last night doing some thinking and it got dark on me. I didn't bring a lantern or anything. I wondered how long it would take me to get back in the dark when they just appeared and lit my path. They stayed until I didn't need them anymore."

"They?"

"Yes, they. What you are seeing is a large group of fireflies. Their butts blink."

Chest rumbling and an open smile on her face, she laughed with him as he repeated, their butts blink. *It sounded too funny not to.* *"Well, it's magnificent. They mimic blinking stars among the trees."*

"Yes they do. They almost blot out the stars altogether."

"Not to ruin the moment, but what had you deep in thought?"

Oh, kissing again. Must have been a good thought. Oh, no, wait more than kissing. *Sweat beaded her body from the heat between them, her lips wet from his kisses and her heart raced onward with every touch. Electricity shot down her spine and the fire consumed her. His wet kisses traced a pattern along her collarbone and back, and her core temperature rose so high, she expected the grass to go up in flames. Her breathing quick and heavy, her leg wrapped around his frame, her fingers trailed down his spine and back. She felt his hand move from her hair and he broke the kiss. She caught her breath. With the cool breeze flowing across her, goose flesh covered her skin. She shivered slightly and not from the cold. Out of the corner of her eye, she spied something sparkle as he moved his arm.*

"I love you, Princess, and I always will. Will you marry me?"

Her eyes moved from his face to the sparkling Topaz ring in his hand, and she lost control. Putting her weight on his shoulders, she pushed him on his back and picked up where he'd left off just moments earlier. Her hands moved to the buttons on his shirt, and her lips never left his. Straddling his midsection, buttons undone, she leaned up and ripped his shirt open.

Red could feel her eyes burning with lust. Her hair hung wildly around her face, and she stopped when he touched her. Her head cupped in his hands, he kept her in place and asked a question that threw her.

"Is that a yes, or a distracted no?"

Seeing the matching hunger in his eyes catching her breath, she answered his question, verbally this time. "Yes, most definitely, yes."

Her left hand in his, she felt the cold, gold ring slide down her finger. Moonlit rays danced around her in an array of what seemed magical energy and color. Watching the light play across his face, she dropped her hand and kissed him again. Caught up in the moment, she vaguely remembered the feverish shedding of clothes. Submerged in the spring, she felt the cool water splashing along her fiery skin. Her mind and body reeled from the heat of their bodies entwined. Electric currents shot through her, playing just under the skin. The mixing of steam from the spring and the chilly air swarming around her, she slipped further into the open arms of pleasure. Needful cravings of the wild beast from within unleashed and set loose. She wrapped herself around him in a sitting position. Her ear lobes and chest were wet and hot from the trail of kisses he'd traced several times. Her hand wound tightly in his hair. Soft moans escaped her lips, embracing her newfound paradise. Waves slapped her back and shoulders as her hips began to move setting a rhythmic pace. Grasping another handful of his hair, she pulled his head back, kissing him, exploring his mouth with her tongue and tasting his sweet breath mixed with hers. Her hips moved in stride as his hands grabbed them in a firm grip and she knotted her hands tighter in his mane.

Her frame moved quickly, feeling the stone under her knees and his chest against her back. He picked up momentum. Reaching up, she placed her arms around his neck pressing her back tighter into him, and his deep moans filled her ears. A fiery inferno ignited inside her as she awaited a volcanic eruption. Her shoulder in one of his hands, her waist in the other, she leaned forward when he urged her to. His hot breath played on the nape of her neck as he kissed her and worked his way down her back. Her hands in front of her on the ledge, she leaned into him as his movement got faster and faster. Her hips firmly gripped in both of his hands her moans mixed with his as they reached the peak of their excitement. A colossal size explosion starting at her core, rippled through her body, wave after wave. She swam in a sea of ecstasy leaving her dizzy and lightheaded.

Chest heaving, breathing uneven, she rested against the ledge of the spring. He dropped into a sitting position beside her, catching his own breath. Turning to look at him, she smiled and spoke breathlessly.

"Does that answer satisfy your question?"

"Wow! Yes, and I must say, feel free to answer all my questions that way."

"I love you, Woody. I would love nothing more than to be your wife."

Leaning over, she placed her hands in either side of his face and kissed him. Swinging her leg over him, she sat on his lap and moved letting him know her intention.

"I love you, too. As much as I would like to keep answering this quest—"

"Again!"

Her mouth covered his, keeping him from talking. Wrapping her arms around his neck, she leaned in and pressed her chest against his lips. She felt his lips move on to her breast as he tried to speak once more.

"We need to…"

She smiled when she felt his mouth suck at her breasts, letting her know she'd won. Her hips danced above him in a steady tempo and his body matched her step for step. Pulling away slightly, she stared into his eyes, and seeing the look there, she took over and finished what she had started. Her waist encircled in his arms and he moved her onto the flat ground. Her back in cool grass, his warm body above her, she wrapped herself around him. Tighter and tighter, she clung to him pulling him further into her. Her body bounced and slid across the ground with the weight of his movements. Screams of pleasure escaped her throat and her fingernails embedded in his back. His ragged breath, whispering cravings, filled her ears, fueling her desire, and sending her over the edge. The ocean of ecstasy, deeper and more powerful this time, threatened to drown her. Her body tightened with his as he moved slower and deeper. Clenching her legs around his frame and grabbing his hair, she kissed him as utopia washed over her. It was euphoric!

Her body trapped beneath him and her breathing, heavy and labored, she closed her eyes and enjoyed the sensation. Cool air swept across her bare chest when he moved to lie next to her.

"Oh My Lord, that was great. However, we need to go. We have been gone awhile, now. Our parents will be looking for us, soon, as they all know what I had planned and why. Well, all but this part."

"I know. This has been the best night of my life. You're right. If our mothers know about the proposal, they'll only wait so long before they have to see it for themselves."

Legs wobbly and arms the consistency of jelly, she got off the ground in search of her clothes. Her dress lay a few feet away. Bending down to get the item, she felt him move up behind her. Standing upright, clutching the dress to her skin, she turned to look at him. Placing a hand on his back, she pressed herself into him and kissed him. She felt his hands gently push her away, breaking the kiss.

"You have got to stop that, or we'll never make it back to the castle before dawn. If we make it then."

Her lips on his lobes, hands softly running down his spine, she whispered. "You started it. Too much for you?"

"No. I just want to live long enough to do that whenever I want. If your father has to look for us, I'm a dead man. Especially if that's what he finds us doing."

That is a sobering thought. *"You're right. Let's get dressed and hurry back."*

Stirring under the blankets, she awoke to the sound of Slaine's loud voice in the hallway followed by a meeker one.

"What do you want? Why are you skulking about on this side of the castle? Shouldn't you be making sure the staff is working or something?"

"The staff is doing as they need to be, as am I? It is my job to care for the Queen. This is what I do every morning. I go in, run her bath, stoke the fire, and help her dress for breakfast.

Why is he yelling, Arabella? Blaze jerked the covers back, jumped out of bed, and ran to the door.

Her heart pounded in her ears and shock crossed her face when she opened the door. "What are you doing? Why are you man-handling her? Let go of her at once."

Looking her in the eyes for what seemed like an eternity, he finally let go of Arabella.

"Arabella, are you all right?"

"Yes, My Queen, I'm fine."

Her eyes went from Slaine to the woman. She watched as Arabella cleared her throat and flattened out her dress before looking at her.

"See…not even a wrinkle."

Slaine spoke. "I'm sorry, Arabella. I have just been on edge. I just want to make sure that no one gets in and hurts Blaze."

"We're all concerned with the Queen's safety, My Lord. Blaze, I'll see you at breakfast."

Turning her back to him, she walked into her room. Her body temperature rose even higher due to the anger she felt. She sensed his presence behind her, following her into the room. It was confirmed when the sound of the door banged shut and she heard his remorseful voice.

"Blaze, please don't be angry with me. I was worried for you. I don't ever want anyone or anything to take you from me again."

"Arabella is my friend, not just a maid. "

"I know. I'm sorry. It won't happen again."

Her body spun and she found herself trapped in his arms. Leaning into his embrace for only a second, she brought up her arms and pushed him away gently. Her eyes on his face, she swallowed once, and spoke.

"I'll let this go this one time. Leave it as a bad over-reaction. Don't let it happen again."

"I promise, you'll never see that again."

"Do I smell vanilla and lavender?"

"Yes. I got up early and readied your bath for you. I know how much you like lavender and vanilla. Did I overdo it?"

He looks like a child who was just caught in the candy jar. How can I tell him he overdid it when he looks so innocent?

"No, I'm sure it is fine. It smells wonderful."

"I just thought you might like a bath before we leave for the festival."

"Why would we go there? You don't like the festival."

Cringing at the way it sounded in her ears, she stood, waiting for it to hit his and the feud to begin. Closing her eyes, she stiffened her body and prepared herself for what would come next. *He must be mad. He is completely quiet. I should have worded that differently. It sounded harsh. I didn't mean for it to. I was just taken by surprise.* She opened her eyes and his voice soft and sorrowful broke the lengthy silence.

"I must apologize for many things, it seems. You were right. The festival is a big event for everyone. Again, I ask that you forgive my pompous behavior."

Blaze just about fell over, so surprised by his words. Lunging forward and wrapping her arms around his neck, she kissed his cheek.

"Nothing to forgive, I guess. This has taken a toll on everyone. I have an idea that might make things better, and I'm hoping it might bring back my memories."

Smile on her face and happiness in her heart, she stared at his face and waited for his reaction.

"Really? Does it involve me being this close to you more often? Maybe closer?"

Pulling away, she playfully smacked his arm and led him to the divan. "Focus. I'm being serious."

Sitting down, she held her head high and her back straight waiting for him to join her. Placing a hand on his arm, once he sat down, she told him of her plan.

"I think you should go back to courting me. I assume and hope that we didn't marry for politics. In addition, we didn't just wake up one day and love each other. It was a process. From my perspective, just as I told you last night, you are a stranger to me. Perhaps if I got to know you all over again, I'm confident it will spark my true feelings for you once more. I hope this doesn't hurt your feelings because it isn't meant to."

"I think that's a wonderful idea. If this is what it takes to make you feel comfortable, then baby steps it is. A perfect solution, I think. I tell you what…you hurry with the bath and I'll come to call in one hour and we shall go to the festival."

He seems on board and confident this will work. He jumped from the couch like a good boy receiving a reward and smiled broadly. Leaning into his arms briefly, she gave him a quick goodbye hug, then watched as he hurried to leave the room. He had the door open, his body half way out when he turned and smiled at her.

"I guess this will be our first date, then." He walked out of the room closing the door behind him.

First date? Oh, I guess he means because I don't remember the others. I have to quit freaking over every little thing. Time to get ready. Today is bound to better than yesterday.

Chapter Nine
Comparing Egos

"The last few days have been nice. We have had a few rough spots, but overall, I think we are doing okay. I can't wait for the Fall Feast tomorrow night."

"Yes, I agree. I want to ask you something. I hope you won't be angry with me, but I'm curious and little miffed about it."

"Fine, go ahead." *Miffed? What does he have to be miffed about? I'm the one who has been trying to overlook his haughty attitude.*

"Why do you like being out here so much?"

Blaze turned and stood in front of him and asked a question of her own.

"What do you mean? Are you talking about here in town with the people? Or here as in this small clearing overlooking the village?'

"Yes, here in this place. Both, I guess. This little park overlooking the town where you sit and watch them. I have seen you here many times. Most of the time, they join you, talking, laughing as if they are your friends. The festival has been nice I guess, but why spend so much time with these people?"

"This place? These people? They are *our* people and I love them. They are more than *people* to me. They are *friends* and I know each and every one of them by their precious faces."

"What for? They are nobodies."

"Nobodies?"

The heat of anger, starting at her feet, slowly snaked its way upward like smoke from a fire. Gritting her teeth, she tried to keep her anger in check. She stared at him and kept her mouth closed until she knew she could speak without biting his head off. Taking a cleansing breath trying to smother the fire, she listened to what he had to say.

"I love the fact you care so much, but why? They know their opinion doesn't really count. It will be as we say. What benefits do you get from them since they are beneath us."

She felt her anger grow hotter and hotter, and harder and harder to control. *How do I explain this without calling him a senseless fool?* Inhaling deeply, she worked at calming herself enough to speak.

"It will be as *we* as a kingdom decide. They know I value their opinions very much. These *people*, as you call them, are what makes this kingdom thrive. I wish you could understand that."

He added fuel to the fire. "Wrong! We as in *you and I* are what makes this kingdom thrive."

"No, Slaine. You are wrong. We wouldn't be a kingdom if that was true." Anger close to boiling over, she tightened her muscles trying to keep from lashing out at his arrogance.

"How do you work that out? We are King and Queen. There is no higher authority. We decide how it is run, what laws to enforce, and how each day will turn out. That simple. There is no need for those below us to intercede. We rule and they follow!"

Fingers on the bridge of her nose, breathing increasing, chest, heavy and full of pain, she tried to explain it better. *He isn't getting this. I don't know whether I want to keep explaining it, or just punch him for his haughtiness.*

"Alright, so we do all that. Now what?"

"That's it. What do you mean, *now what?*"

"What happens next?"

"Like I said, we make the rules and tell them what to do and they do it. That is how it works. Don't be stupid."

That's it. That is the last straw! I have heard enough. Anger and fury burst through the surface like an explosion and she fired off at him with both barrels.

"I'm not stupid! First of all, you are completely arrogant. Second, have fun running a kingdom all by yourself because that's all you will have left. That's not a kingdom. It's just a King! Just a small-minded man playing a big role no one cares for. Good luck with that, Slaine!"

Not emptied of her anger and fury, she turned on her heels, and walked away. She managed to take three steps before she felt his grip on her arm pulling her back.

"Wait. I apologize. Please stop."

She spun on her heels and looked straight into those spine-chilling eyes, and for once, she didn't fear what shone there. Her body filled with anger and fury, slowly turning to hatred and disgust. This time, fear, a long ago memory, now sat below the honor of her people and kingdom.

"For what?"

"For calling you stupid, I crossed the line. I lost my temper. I see your point. I just disagree with it."

"Then, we will have to agree to disagree. I won't stop spending time with them. I value each and every one of them. To me, they are as vital to this kingdom as we are. I, for one, would like to know who's a part of this kingdom and who's happy and unhappy. Unhappiness is a poison that stalks like a snake hunting in the grass. Slowly moving, undetected, watching its prey, and when the first opportunity rises, it strikes at its unsuspecting victim, soon devouring it, whole."

"I don't understand. I mean I understand the analogy, but I just don't see how it applies here."

"Take your body for instance. Say, it represents the Kingdom…" She moved her hands above his frame to help emphasize her point. "Your big head will represent the King. Inside the body are these people. They get unhappy. The poison starts small, in just the arm, but soon spreads throughout the entire body. What happens, then? The body…the Kingdom dies. Then all you're left with is that big empty head. A kingdom can't function with just the head."

"Your theory is nice, and now let me tell you mine. My head, the King, makes all the decisions. I tell my body what to do and it responds to my commands. I want my leg to move and it does. It's as simple as that."

Just look at the smug smile. He thinks he has it all figured out. Holy spirits! What is Demarko doing here? Is he asking to get his head chopped off? Oh, great and he is going to speak to Slaine.

"What you say is true, My Lord."

Her head moving from side to side as if watching a ball-tossing match, she stared in shock and hoped for the best.

"However, My Lord, the Queen does present a sound theory. While both are true, yours just won't work for long."

"How so?"

"Demarko, it's okay. Thank you for your insight. How about I catch up with you later and we can talk some more." *Please leave. The more he talks, the angrier Slaine gets. His face has already changed colors three times. Why is Demarko pushing his luck?*

"No, no. Let him stay. I would love to hear this."

Look at him standing there so handsome and stupid. Does he think this will win some points? Anger turned to worry. *I'm all for honor, but this is madness.* Her heart started a marathon race. *I swear, all Slaine needs is a half-bad excuse to kill him. He won't admit to it, but it's written on his face and in his demeanor every time Demarko's name is just mentioned.* Ragged breaths escaped her lungs with her labored breathing. *It's worse when he's around. Great, Demarko isn't leaving and he looks as if he is going to open his mouth again.* Sweat beaded her brow and the sound of his voice left her light headed.

"Well, it's true, your leg will move when you tell it to. Your eyes will focus when you ask, and your mouth will speak when you think you have something to say. Here is where the kink in your theory begins. The Queen's method has a built-in preventive. Having that open relationship and trust, when the people have a problem, they will act on that by addressing the Queen. Blaze will work with them to find an agreeable solution. They might not get exactly what they want, but they will get something they can live with. Therefore, you see, having that is like having a vaccine that repels the poison keeping it from spreading or even getting a good hold. You can't keep yourself from being sick simply because you will it. Illnesses happen. That is why a preventive is needed, or at least an antidote to cure it."

Holding her breath, she watched them both as Demarko spoke. When he was done, Slaine looked crazed, waving his arms in the air and ranting like a mad man.

"I should have known you would take her side. Everybody takes her side."

"This isn't about taking sides. It's about seeing the truth between a theory and a fact. You had a theory, but hers is a proven fact. If you want proof, all you have to do is ask the villagers."

She felt helpless as she continued to watch it unfold. Her heart beat like a hammer against her chest and she felt it pulse in her neck. Her breathing quick and heavy, she thought, she might pass out, or start hyperventilating. *This isn't good. Why couldn't he just leave. I could handle this. Slaine is getting madder by the second. His face is scarlet, his body is tense and looks like a viper about to strike. Now, it begins. I hope yelling is as far as it goes. If not, I'm going to have to think of an escape plan for Demarko.*

She stood and watched as Slaine's fury erupted and spilled out, his loud opinion filling the air.

"How dare you come up here and invade our time together. Who do you think you are? We will see who you agree with when I'm finished with you."

I can't allow this. Taking a chance, she stepped between the two men and hoped to diffuse the situation. "Demarko, what are you doing up here, anyway?"

"I was in town delivering messages and I had a message for you, so I came up here. I was caught up in the conversation. I was only trying to help."

Standing in front of Demarko, hand on his chest, she asked him another question and wished for Slaine to calm down, or leave. "What was the message?"

"Arabella is looking for you." He lowered his voice. "Why are you standing in my way? I'm not afraid of him. Please move. I don't want you to get hurt. It's not my fault that he's ignorant to the way things are."

Her feet moved her body quickly when he nudged her out of the way. She stood staring at them both, hoping and praying it didn't escalate any further. *Men! I am trying to keep the peace and they want to compare egos. Fine!* Moving a few more feet away, she kept her eye on both of them, barely breathing. *I can't let him get himself hurt for the sake of egos or being right, or whatever he is thinking.* Stepping back to Demarko, she placed her hand on his arm and looked into his beautiful eyes.

"Thank you for the message, Demarko. I will find her soon. You may go."

"No, I'm not sure now is a good time. He still looks too angry. I worry for your safety."

"As your Queen, that is an order and I expect it to be followed."

Looking him in the face, she felt his muscles flex under her hand. He was hesitant to leave so she whispered her plea.

"Please, Demarko, your presence here is only making it worse. I don't know why he hates you so, but he does. Please go."

Locked into his gaze for only a moment, he pulled away and walked off. She closed her eyes and felt a sigh of relief. When she turned to look at Slaine, she hoped, she hadn't made a terrible mistake. *Well, he doesn't look any happier.*

"You're both wrong. I have tried to plead with you and now I demand you to stay away from them. All of them, they're but dirt under our shoes and I won't have my wife fraternizing with such slime."

"You think that just because you are King that you are somehow better than these people? I can't believe after all you have seen, you could still feel that way. These people—*our* people—love us, and this kingdom. It's our duty to treat them fairly. The fact that I genuinely love each one of them is a bonus. I can't imagine how we ended up married. We are nothing alike. Our views are totally different, major issues."

"We married because we love each other. As for the rest, we *are* better than they are. As King and Queen, it is our duty to rule them, and nothing more. They live to serve us and not the other way around, Blaze."

She closed her eyes. "God please forgive this ignorant man." Taking a deep breath, she eyed the dimwit in front of her. "As for love, Slaine, I can't possibly love one such as you. You're arrogant, rude, and downright hateful."

Wonderful. As if one giant ass isn't enough. Oh, and here he goes, opening his mouth and letting loose his repulsive tone. I know this is only going to get worse. I'm glad Demarko is not here. He would end up dead, I'm sure of it.

"Well, that is no way to speak to your King and master."

Blaze turned her head towards the sound of the new voice and recognized Deklan. Rolling her eyes and letting out her breath, she wondered how long he would be here this time.

"Brother, are you going to let her talk to you that way? Who runs this place, you or her? I thought it was you since you are the King, but obviously I was wrong."

"You're right, Deklan. I am her King and master."

He looks like a blowfish when he bows out his chest. Here it comes once again. Time to tighten the jaw because I'm not backing down. I refuse to give them the satisfaction of seeing me cower down or beg him to stop. Maybe, if it would stop them, but it won't.

Three small breaths was all it took and he was in her face.

"I won't allow you speaking to me that way. I demand an apology, right now!"

"I will no—"Her cheeks and jaw felt the burn first. Her eyes blurred and went out of focus as her body dropped onto the earth. Palms and knees on the ground, head throbbing from pain, she cleared her watery vision and got up. Standing tall, she glared at them both.

"Feel better, now? Does that make you feel like a big powerful man?"

"Blaze, it doesn't make me feel better. I wish you wouldn't push me to that point. No, you aren't leaving. I'm not done talking to you."

"I'm done talking to *you*. Unless you feel like smacking me again, of course. Hey, why not let Deklan in on the fun? He's dying to try it."

Her glare darted from one to the other. Nobody moved, but she noticed a slight twitch in Deklan's hand. "No? Fine."

Jerking her arm out of his grip with tears in her eyes, she turned and walked toward the castle. The sound of arrogant laughter and snide comments echoed behind her as she stormed away. Once inside, she rushed past everyone to get to her room. Her feet carried her quickly down the hall and through the door to her room. Pacing back and forth, she absent mindedly rubbed her face and jumped when someone knocked on the door.

"Who is it?"

"It's Arabella. I saw you come into the castle, upset. May I come in?"

Thank God it's her. Tears still dropping from her cheeks, breathing uneven and hands shaking, she opened the door and engulfed the woman in a hug. "Thank the Lord above, it's you. I could use a friend right now."

Pulling away from the woman, she stepped around and closed the door.

"Come, sit, and tell me what happened."

Walking toward the end of her room, she dropped onto the divan and cleared her throat of sobs so she could explain.

"Slaine is impossible and arrogant! He is so unlike me..." A fiery rage ignited once more. "He has no compassion for our people and gets violently angry because I do. It's infuriating! He actually thinks he is better than they are becau—"

"What is that on your face? Did he slap you?"

A warm soft hand touched the handprint clearly left there and fresh tears spilled out. Closing her eyes, she focused on the soothing warmth as it pushed away the hurt. Face in the woman's palm, her cheek felt better and the pain faded away. She felt the woman drop her hand, but the warmth of her touch lingered like the scent of flowers in the air. Opening her eyes slowly, she wiped the fresh tears away and looked into Arabella's sorrowful face.

"No need to answer that the proof is there. So, what caused this?"

"Slaine and I were arguing. He wants me to stop being with my people and I refused. When Demarko showed up, he really got angry. I made him leave, but he was still mad. Then, Deklan showed up and you know how that goes. Anytime he is around, Slaine always gets violent. You know, the usual, I guess."

"I'm sorry that he struck you. I wish there was something I could do to prevent this from happening again."

Looking at Arabella with tears in her eyes only made her feel worse. Her breaking heart and ragged breaths only fueled the hurt and fanned the fire of fury. She leapt from the small couch and started pacing.

"There's nothing to be done. Slaine thinks he's the highest authority around here. Deklan is no help. He encourages it because he feels the same way. Deklan struts around here as if he owns the place. And why not? He knows Slaine will lash out at anyone who crosses him. Just last week, Slaine had Mr. Trent hanged. Deklan said he overheard the man talking of treason. I was unable to save him. Slaine struck me then, too. I tried so hard to get to him, but Deklan held me back with his hand over my mouth to quiet my screams. He kept me from being able to go into the entrance hall and prevent Slaine from giving the guards the orders to kill him. When I lashed out at Slaine for not giving the man a fair trial first was when he hit me. When I was in the village the other day, two of the villagers informed me Frank got into a fight with Deklan because he was trying to have his way with Frank's wife. So, what happens? Deklan got his butt kicked and then ran to Slaine and said he was ambushed and demanded he be hanged."

"What happened after that?"

"When Slaine and his guards came for the man, the villagers said he tucked tail and ran, taking his family with him. Deklan was furious. When I questioned him about it, he got angry and told me it was none of my business. Naturally, I disagreed. It ended with me on the floor and Deklan laughing encouragements. There's so much more that they have done I haven't questioned them about. He thinks he is hiding it, or maybe he just doesn't care. I don't care what the consequences are. I will stand up for this kingdom and everybody in it."

"I know, dear. I'm sorry."

"It's all right." She dropped onto the sofa. "I know that you need to get back to the staff. I will be fine. My feelings are what hurt the most, not my face. Here, I'll walk you to the door."

She hugged her best friend. Once she pulled away, she walked her to the wooden door. Hand on the frame, she hugged her once more.

Bang. Bang. Bang.

"That would be Slaine, no doubt."

"Don't push it with him. Maybe you should do as he says so that he won't strike you again—just until we figure out how to fix this."

Bang. Bang. Bang.

"Perhaps if you act like you're not here, he'll go away."

"No need for that. I'm sure he's been listening to the whole conversation. I have noted that he stands on the other side of the door, the one almost hidden by the bookshelf and listens to what is going on in my room…"

Leaning over the woman and lowering her voice, she whispered the last of her conversation.

"Or, he has Deklan stand on the other side of that door. They're not as quiet as they think."

"I see."

Bang. Bang. Bang.

Steadying her nerves, taking a deep breath, and exhaling, she opened the door to face the man she despised.

"What do you want, Slaine?"

"What's she doing here?"

"I was just leaving, My Lord."

She moved between Slaine and Arabella so her friend could leave the room unscathed. "Must you be rude to everyone? Why aren't you playing with Deklan…he steal one of your toys?"

Dropping her hand from the door, she turned and walked away from him. *What does he want, to bore me some more? Argue again? Oh, I bet he is here to say he is sorry. And, he is right! He is sorry. He's always the sorriest when his brother isn't around. I wonder what excuse he will use this time.*

Slouching on the divan, she tapped her foot and traced her fingernails as if he weren't there. Her face now painless, her body numb, she simply didn't care. Leaning her head back, arm in the air, she looked at her hand in different angles and waited for his annoying mouth to open and his excuses to begin.

"Please forgive me. I'm sorry."

"Why, whatever for?" She leaned up and glared at him. "You have the right to treat me however you please, you know, since you're the master of the universe. Unfortunately for me, I am stuck here with you."

"Please, Blaze."

"Why? Why did you do it?"

"You just made me so angry, and Deklan was there…I am sorry. Please forgive me, Blaze. I love you and I hate myself for what I did."

She kept an eye on him as he dropped to his knees, hanging his head.

"Please. Please say you forgive me."

What would it change…nothing. It will just happen again. That apparently is just who he is. I just want him to go. Maybe if I say what he wants to hear, he will leave me alone for a while.

"Fine. I forgive you."

"Thank you, Blaze. I love you and I never want to hurt you."

Eyes focused on the fool on the floor, she watched him get up and lean her way. *Oh, dear God, I hope he doesn't think we are going to kiss and make up. I'm not sure I have the strength for another fight today.*

Body stiff, she held her breath and waited to see where he kissed her. Cheeks warm with his touch, he pulled her close. She reached up and placed her hands on his arms. Ready to push his advance in the opposite direction, she noticed he closed his eyes and kissed her. *Whew. That was close. Only on the forehead. I hope that he leaves now.* Exhaling a sigh of relief, she let her body relax a little as he leaned away. Heart rate slowing, her fiery rage burning out, and she felt herself fill with something else...*weariness.*

"Will you join me for the Fall Feast Banquet?"

"Yes."

"Thank you. I will be here shortly before sunset to walk you in."

She tried half-heartedly to keep the sarcasm out of her voice, but failed. "I will be ready and waiting."

Finally, he's gone. I think I'm going to lock the door and go to sleep. I'm exhausted from all of this. At least he won't be back until sunset tomorrow.

Locking the door and walking back to her bed, she pulled back the blanket and lay down. Heavy eyes and exhausted body, she quickly drifted off to another land containing a better life...

Red nestled into his embrace. Head on his shoulder, hands entwined with his, she closed her eyes and enjoyed the few minutes of stolen peace from all the activity. Her mind raced. She tried to slow it down, but the events of the last few months replayed in her mind.

Everyone was busy doing something. Shaunt, after getting the guest list, sent out invitations and messages to the surrounding villages. He even had to recruit some of the town's people for help with finding material for dresses, decorations, messages for seamstresses, and formal invitations for bands and entertainment. Arabella had been to the local markets looking for food and supplies for the wedding feast and even snatched a female cook from the Inn Dever to help. She and Woody had been knee deep in fabrics swatches, flowers, and colors. Their mothers were relentless. Their fathers were on a hunting trip, trapping and gathering game for the feast as well as overseeing renovations on the castle. All was to be perfect.

"This is nice..."

"And peaceful. Finally, a few moments away from all the hustle and bustle. Not to mention... Here they come."

Footsteps sounded in her ears for just a moment before they stopped. Opening her eyes, she looked up into the expectant faces of her mother and Woody's mother, Erianna.

"Just a few quick questions and I promise we'll leave you two alone for a while."

"Red, would you like some roses in your bouquet and if so, what color and how many? The headpiece has Pedalstem Lillies. Would you also like Baby's Breath and Lavender? Finally, would you like to enter from the entrance hall doors or descend from the stairs?"

"A few roses with big Pedalstem Lillies accented with Lavender for the bouquet. I want Lavender added to the veil, also with a small amount of Baby's Breath. Father will want to descend from the stairs."

"Your turn, Son. Would you like a lily or a rose on your lapel and if so, do you want it to match her bouquet or veil? Would you like to enter the room from behind the altar at the same time as Red, or be standing and waiting for her?"

"A single Pedalstem Lilly as it's Red's favorite and I'll be waiting at the altar. Anything else, Mother?"

"Nope, that's all. We'll handle the rest. We have special plans and the two of you need to be out of our way so that we can finish them without your knowledge."

Her eyes followed the two women as they walked out of the garden, acting suspicious. I'm so exhausted, I don't even care what they are planning. *Leaning against him once more, head back on his shoulder, she breathed a sigh of relief.*

"Finally, I feared when they came in here we were going to be dragged off to do something. My body is completely drained. We've been moving, planning, and working from sun up to sun down for almost six months. I can't wait until tomorrow. I get light headed just thinking about it."

"Me, too! I'm glad it is finally here. Maybe we can get some rest. After tonight, we'll be in the same bed. I'm looking forward to *that. Being able to fall asleep each night with you in my arms is my dream come true. "*

"Mine, too. My bed will never be cold again and if it ever is...well I have someone to help me warm it up."

"Yes. A place where you can answer all my questions."

She giggled with him at their private joke and reveled in all the fun ways she could do just that. Palms on his chest, she pushed up enough to look him in the face. Leaning up, she kissed him.

"Yes, and answer all your questions. Just as I did when you asked me to marry you. If my body wasn't so tired and refusing to move, I would answer the question playing in your mind right now."

Smiling at his expression, she leaned back against his chest and rested her head on his shoulder. Her body vibrated with his laughter. His soft-spoken words tickled the fine hairs on her ears.

"And what question would that be? I'm sure I have no idea to what you are referring."

"You want to know if we have enough time to run off so we can answer questions in the hot spring again. So foul minded."

"Ah, you got me. I'm caught. However, I'm not the only foul minded one. If you weren't as well, you wouldn't know what I was thinking and you wouldn't be smiling and trying to hide that flush on your cheeks."

"Am not! I just know you, that's all."

"Ah-huh. Lie all you want, but I know you well enough to know that you were thinking the same as I."

"You're right, but I'm so tired. I admit I had planned to try and sneak off with you, but my exhaustion is having different ideas."

Nestling her body closer, she brought her arms near her chest and felt his breath move her hair slightly when he spoke.

"I'm tired, too."

Her frame shook with a small tremor as a slight chill danced across her. She felt him pull her close and kiss her head. Warmth soaking into her skin, she closed her eyes and soon fell asleep. Soon, too soon. Twisting her frame, she pressed harder into him trying to block out the breeze. Her eyes fluttered with the haze from her nap as she opened them. Shadows and low light blinked in and out of sight, she brought her hand up and wiped the sleep from her eyes. Her body moved underneath his as he awoke and moved. A loud booming laugh filled her ears, but, she felt no vibrations rustle her frame.

"Huh?"

Her frame suddenly lunged forward and Red almost landed on the ground. Her arms in his hands kept her from seeing the grass close up. Turning her head, she looked at him to see why he had jumped when he spoke.

"What do we need to do? I'm sorry that we fell asleep."

Red followed his gaze and saw her father, her mother, and both of his parents standing in front of them wearing big smiles, trying to hide the laughter in their voices. Her father broke the tense silence first.

"Simmer down. No one is in any trouble."

"We were just commenting on how cute the two of you look. Red, it is ladies' time. Woody, you're to go with the men."

Her hand suddenly in her mother's, putting weight on her legs, she stood. Looking over her shoulder, she glanced at Woody sitting on the bench who just shrugged. No way out of this! Turning back, she noticed her mother's arm pointing towards the setting sun.

"It's officially night fall. Bad luck to see the bride before the wedding. So, off with the men folk."

"Shoo, shoo," Erianna said.

Blaze's body shook with laughter, chasing away the last bit of sleepiness as she watched Erianna pushing on the men's backs, helping them to move out of the garden. Silk fabric rubbed her arm and she turned to see her mother holding something out for her.

"Here, slip into your bathing attire. We shall sit in the spring, have wine, and some woman talk."

Hands under her dress, she grabbed her under things, slid them off, and dropped them on the bench behind her. Bathing attire in hand, she fed her legs through, pulled it up half way, and stopped at her stomach. Hand crossed on each side of her dress, she pulled it off and dropped it on top of her under things. Quickly, she reached down and finished putting on the bathing attire. Suit in place, she padded along the grass and joined her mother, Arabella, and Erianna in the hot spring. Glass in hand, filled with wine, she sipped it slowly as she listened to the conversation. As if I need the *what to expect on my wedding night* speech. Oh, Lord, I can't believe they just mentioned that. I think I might need more wine.

Blush crossed her cheeks, heat reddened her face, and she emptied the glass of its contents when her mother asked the question she'd hoped wouldn't come up.

"So, have you and Woody practiced for the private show?"

Good Lord! How can I answer this, better yet, how should I answer this? If it were just my mother, I would just tell her, but his mother is here, too. Then, of course, Arabella is, too. She knows the answer. Would she tell them if I lied? *Body frozen in place, eyes wide and watching, she glanced from one face to another. They all had the same expression upon their faces. The look that said, We're waiting. Swallowing hard, she forced herself to gain control of her nerves and answered their question.*

"Yes. We have practiced, as you put it, a few times."

Closing her eyes and putting her hands in front of her face, she waited for the you should have waited for your wedding night *sermon to begin. Slowly, she dropped her hands and opened her eyes. She eyed each face and no one said anything.* Am I to get away with this? God, I hope so.

"I guess I should be upset, but since you are to be wed in a few hours, I suppose I could let it go. But you have to answer one question for me."

Lord, this could go both ways. Could be good, but most likely, it is going be embarrassing. *"Alright, what's the question? Wait. I have a feeling I may need more wine."*

"Arabella, will you fill her glass, please. I have the same feeling and I'm not the one asking the question. Yet, I know what it will be. Drink up, Red," Erianna said.

Hand shaking, spilling some of its contents, she looked at her mother. Once seeing her expression, she turned the glass up and finished it. Stretching out her arm, she tapped the glass on Arabella's shoulder indicating she wanted a refill. Glass refilled, she motioned for her mother to ask away.

"So, what was it like? I mean did you like it?"

It had to be that question, didn't it? Of course it did. Oh, my! *Choking on her mother's question, most likely, she coughed until her throat cleared. Sweat beaded her brow and ran down her back. Her heart and pulse raced to an imaginary finish line. She stared into her mother's face.*

"It's perfectly fine, dear. You can answer the question. I know, he's my son, but I, too am just interested in the fact that it won't be an issue. We aren't looking for details, just a reassurance that we don't need to give advice about pointers and such."

Her mother chimed in, "That's a very important part of any marriage. Let me restate the question. When you are together, what do you feel? Love, desire, or is it just young raw lust?"

"Well, yes. I mean, no...wait let me begin anew. It's all that and more. There is lust, desire, need, but mostly I can feel love from both of us. There will be no problems in that area."

Dropping her eyes from each mother, she tightened her grip on her wine glass and sipped it to have something to do besides look embarrassed. That was awkward and weird. I hope that is the worst of it. Thank God for Arabella. I think she is going to bail me out of this embarrassment.

"Okay, now I think we have embarrassed the poor girl enough for one night. How about we lighten the air and talk of other woman things. Perhaps maybe old boyfriends or fun times we have had."

"She does look a bit pale. If she faints and drowns, my son will never forgive me, well us. If I fall from grace, Kathryn, I am taking you with me," Erianna pointed out, with a wicked grin on her face.

"Well, that wouldn't be a first. You were always dragging me into some kind of trouble when we were young," protested her mother.

Erianna fired back, "I beg your pardon. I was the good one. You were the one getting me into trouble."

Arabella joined the fun, "Wait, wait. If my memory serves me correctly, the two of you were thick as thieves and getting each other in trouble. You were each other's partners in crime. Then when Fayne and Ashton came along—"

"Well, we all know your memory is slipping, old woman. No need to tell your version of the story," Woody's mother playfully snapped back.

Laughter from the three women filled the air. Head still, both hands on her glass, she sipped her wine and watched them go back and forth at each other. Her eyes darted from one face to another like a three-person tennis match. Her nerves calmed and her body relaxed, she found herself caught up in the friendly banter, and laughed with them. This is better. Nice to know that our parents were just as crazy as we are. Well, actually they were worse. Woody and I never snuck out to attend a gala where we were not allowed. Never stole wine from the kitchen either. Wow, this is fun. I am glad they are finished focusing on my indiscretions. *Her mother, acting as the voice of reason, caught her attention.*

"Well, we need to get her to bed soon it is almost light out. Come on, Red I will, help you to bed."

"I'm sure I can make it. You can walk with me if you want. I haven't had that much wine."

"Okay, if you say so. Lead the way, dear."

Setting the glass on the ground behind her, Blaze stood up, intent on getting out. A rush of light-headedness took over, leaving her dizzy and unable to stand properly. Water splashed her face as her body dropped back onto the ledge and she burst out laughing.

"Maybe I should, help you, Mother. You look a bit off."

"That's because you are sitting sideways in the water while the rest of us are standing on the bank. Maybe you shouldn't have stolen that bottle of wine when you thought we weren't looking."

Her arms held up by Erianna and her mother, she stood on uncooperative limbs. Concentrating on the task, she stood a little straighter and walked out of the spring. "I'm fine now. A little fuzzy-brained, but I can walk. I just stood up too fast."

Erianna asked concerned "Are you sure?"

"Yes. I probably couldn't run a marathon, but I can walk."

Right arm locked with her mother and the left locked with Erianna, she laughed at nothing in particular as they walked to her room.

Chapter Ten
The Fall Feast

Cheeks blushed pink, eyes brushed in a light teal, and lips glossed, she double-checked her make up in the mirror. *Perfect!* Hands pulling at her soft red spirals, she fixed her hair and added a small peacock feather, clipping the sides together nicely in the back. Turning her head from left to right, Blaze glanced to be sure her hair was in proper order. *Tonight's the big night. Oh, I'm so excited. I can't wait to see all the townies in their new fresh outfits we made.*

Stepping back and slightly turning her frame this way and that, she smoothed out her gown and looked at herself in the mirror. Long and elegant, it went all the way to her toes. It was a beautiful teal color with a one-inch seam done in peacock feathers. *This has to be my favorite gown. I love the peacock theme for this year's Fall Feast!* Reaching over and grabbing her bracelet, she heard a knock at the door.

"Be right there."

Placing the bangle on her wrists, she turned to answer the door and noticed Slaine was standing in the doorway.

"Oops, sorry. The door just fell open. Would you like for me to close it back, or can I at least enjoy the view?"

He is almost attractive when he is charming. Trying to keep the smile from her face, she looked at him. Hair slicked back and neat, His face wore a sly smile, which lessened the threat in his eyes. He

145

leaned against the frame of the door bunching up his tight red silk shirt. His legs crossed at the ankle as he leaned, creased the form-fitting black pants. When he moved to advance into the room, his new dark leather boots squeaked a bit.

"Hmm...I will have someone come fix that door. I can't have it falling open all the time. Next time, I might be in the middle of dressing or something. The staff would get an eye full, then."

"Oh, I don't think that's necessary. I think the door just can't resist my big personality and can't keep from falling open to me."

His laughter filled her ears and she smiled. "I think it's your big ego pushing on the door while your hands help to undo the latch."

Looping her arm through his, she let him lead her out the door and toward the banquet hall.

"You look beautiful, Blaze. I'm the luckiest guy in the whole kingdom."

"Thank you. You don't look half-bad yourself. I'm glad you like the outfit."

Well, here he comes to ruin our nice conversation. Good God, it is getting harder and harder to play polite. I wish Deklan would leave already.

"Well, don't you look debonair?"

"Thank you, brother. You look nice yourself. Blaze does nice work with fabric doesn't, she?"

"Yes, she does. Thank you again, Blaze for the new robes."

"Don't mention it. Where did you come from? I didn't see you."

"I was standing right there. Slaine asked me to meet him here. The three of us are walking in together."

She turned her disappointed glare toward Slaine. Once again, he fashioned an excuse for his brother to be with them.

"I told Deklan to meet us at the end of the hall next to the large pillar. He's new, still. I didn't want him to have to walk in alone."

New? He has been here for almost a year. Havoc and all.

"Fine. Let's go. The people are waiting."

"Um, Brother, we need to talk a minute before we go in."

"Can it wait, Deklan? Now isn't the time."

Looking from face to face, Blaze saw Slaine nod his head

slightly in her direction. *What are they up to now? Can't they be civil for one night?*

"Our little problem... Did you fix it?"

She questioned them. "What problem?"

"No worries. No worries. It doesn't concern you, sweetheart. It'll only be a minute while I wrap this insignificant little detail up."

"Well, Slaine? Did it happen or not?" Deklan asked, a little aggravation in his tone.

"It didn't go as planned, so it's still...around."

"Obviously, you two think this has to be done now. So, how about I just meet you in the banquet hall?"

Pulling her arm from his, she turned and walked away. Three steps from the brothers, she heard Demarko's name. Pausing shortly, one foot off the ground, she contemplated confronting them. Putting her foot back and resuming her strides, she continued to the hall and to her awaiting people. Palms flat upon each door, she paused to clear her head of the bad vibes and placed a huge smile upon her face.

Pushing open the door, she saw a beautiful hall filled with light, sound, and the smell of fresh food and flowers. The tables were draped in cream-colored runners. A soft glow illuminated off the small mirrors that held teal and purple candles. In the center of each table, a large vase filled with Pedalstem Lillies, arranged beautifully, accented with one long peacock feather. Loud music played from the platform, which once held the thrones and now held a small band. People dotted the room, dancing, singing, and talking with one another. It was loud, it was busy, and it was fun!

Walking past the band unaware of him, Shaunt scooped her up and swung her out on the floor for her first dance. Her hand in his and her waist cupped with his other, they twirled around the floor. Leaning forward and back, kicking their feet here and there, she laughed aloud as he spun her in circles around the other guests. The room filled with laughter, *yeahs*, and the occasional *show off* floated through the air as they made their final trip around the room. Hand on her chest and beads of sweat glistening on her forehead, she sat down to catch her breath.

"Whew, that was fun. Thank you, Shaunt. I'm surprised I remembered how to do that."

"Dancing is like walking...once you learn, you never really forget."

Her hand in his, he kissed it once, bowed slowly, and spoke softly. "I shall see you in a while, My Queen. I need to check on some errands."

Nodding to him, she smiled and watched him walk away. Lifting her hand to her brow, she pushed a few strands of hair out of her face and noticed Slaine sit down next to her.

"Did you have fun with the old man?"

"Yes, I did. Who knotted your kilt?" *Should have known he would be brooding again. He always finds a reason.*

"What's that supposed to mean?"

"Well, you are mad about something. What is it this time?"

"I don't like seeing you dance with other men."

Slapping her hand on the table and turning half way around to face him, she glared at his face and felt her body, heat up as it filled with agitation.

"Oh, for, heaven's sake! He's a good friend. You need to realize, I'm the Queen and I can't tell my people *no* if they ask to dance with me. It's impolite. That's the reason for this celebration, us coming together as a kingdom, as equals. I'm sorry you don't like it, but you will have to find a way to deal with it. No one is crossing a line here but you!"

"Always so flippant and defiant! Can't you just do what I tell you! Must you embarrass and be rude to me at every turn?"

"Must you be so arrogant, and maybe ask instead of order? You will find I'm much more cooperative if you ask."

"Fine! Will you *please* not dance with anyone else?"

"No! This is a celebration and we are supposed to dance. You know if you tried it, I bet you would find that you like it."

An idea struck her as she thought to soften the situation. Holding out her hand, she reached for his. "Come on, I will show you."

Feeling the sting in her hand when he slapped it away, she dropped it and stopped talking to him.

"I won't go out there and look like a fool."

Hair blew away from her face when he jumped out of his chair and walked away. Crossing her arms on her chest, she fought back tears that threatened to fall and would certainly ruin her makeup. *I'm not going to cry. I spent an excessive amount of time in front of that mirror putting this stuff on my face. Let him brood! I'm here to show this kingdom a good time and I mean to have a great time!* Hands flat in the table, she pushed herself up and got out of her chair. Looking around the room, she decided to mingle. Halfway around the table, she heard her name from behind her. Turning, she saw Mrs. Willow smiling at her.

"Hello, Mrs. Willow. Are you enjoying the evening? I have to say, loving that dress…it fits you well."

"Thank you, My Queen."

"No need for that tonight. Save the bowing and formalities for business."

"As you wish. I'm having a great time. You have done a wonderful job with the decorations. The food smells…well, it's making my mouth water, I can't wait to taste it. So, I hear rumor, My Queen, that the meat vendor prepared tonight's meal?"

"No. Arabella and the staff cooked tonight's meal. They have been working for days to get it as close to perfection as they can."

"Well, I'll have to go tell Mrs. Nosey Rosey, she had it wrong, then. I bet she was even wrong when she said the King's brother has been doing terrible things in the village. I knew she was lying. I told her that you wouldn't allow such things to happen here."

"Thank you for the confidence. I'll go and speak to Nos—I mean Rose—about this in the morning. For now, we're here to have a good time. Why haven't I seen you on the dance floor with some handsome man?"

Smile on her face, laughter in her throat, she looked at the blush crossing the woman's face as she explained.

"Well, I…I can't. I mean I don't…I can't dance, My Queen. I'm sorry to disappoint you."

149

"Nonsense. Anyone can dance. You just need the right teacher. Come, give me your hand. I know just the person."

"Really. I have never danced before."

"Wait! You have never danced before?"

"Not even with my late husband. We met here at the feast many years ago, but we never danced. Since he has passed on, I just haven't thought to ask anyone. I'm old now."

"Well, if you don't mind, you're going to dance tonight."

"Actually, now that I'm going to, I feel like a young girl. I am so giddy. Lead the way."

Arm in arm, she held the woman's hand and led her to the end of the hall. She had him in her sights and was determined to have this woman dance. Her hand in the air about to tap him on the shoulder, he whisked Rosemarie out onto the dance floor.

"Well, that's all right, My Lady. I'll just dance later. Thank you anyway."

"He will be—"

"I don't mean to intrude, My Lady. But I do believe that I can, help."

"Is that right, Demarko?"

Her body heat rose and her palms got sweaty as she looked at his well-built frame and let his voice fill her ears. *He looks so handsome. Black coat and pants stitched in gold. It was my favorite outfit to make and he looks better than I pictured.* Trying to keep her breathing even, she watched as he took Mrs. Willows' hand and spoke to her.

"Let me show you how it's done. I bet we can out dance them. What do you say?"

"Oh, I will give it a try."

Hand over her face, she tried to keep her laughter to herself when she saw Mrs. Willow pinch his butt and Demarko's face go from tan to scarlet in the length of a heartbeat.

"It's always nice to see your Queen smiling and having a good time."

"Hello, Kip. Thank you."

"What's so funny?"

"I brought Mrs. Willows over to dance with Shaunt, but he was already out on the floor with Rosemarie, so Demarko asked her to dance. He was leading her to the dance floor and she reached up and pinched his butt. He jumped as if someone scared him. You should have seen his face. It turned red, then scarlet. I think he might have been a bit embarrassed."

"I always say it is the old ones you have to worry about."

Slapping his wrist and laughing, she kind-heartedly reprimanded him.

"Stop. You be nice."

"What? I'm always nice, but it's true. Older women will tell it to you straight."

"You just be on your best behavior. Here they come."

"Oh, my. That was exciting. Thank you, Demarko."

"I think I would like to dance. My Lady, will you join me?"

Extending her hand and smiling broadly, she returned his bow. "Why thank you, Kip. I accept."

Hand on his arm, following him onto the floor, she stopped when she heard her name called. As she turned around, she saw a short young woman standing there.

"Yes?"

"Arabella would like to see you."

"Thank you, Maize. Tell her that after I dance with Kip, I will be right there."

"Okay. "

Turning her attention back to Kip, she said, "Shall we?"

"Yes, My Lady."

Body twirling round and round, she kept her eyes on Kip to keep the dizziness at bay. She smiled and laughed along with him. Her frame stayed straight as they moved while her feet stepped forward and back as they waltzed around the floor.

"This is nice. Who taught you to dance?"

"My mother."

"Well, I must say, I loved dancing with Shaunt, but I prefer this slower pace. It is easier to talk, visit, and just enjoy the evening."

"I'm glad that you approve, My Queen."

Arm in the air and fingers gently lying in his hand, he twirled her back to the sideline. Her dress crumpled in her hand, pulling it up slightly, and dropping her head, she bowed to him in thanks.

"Thank you, My Queen, for the dance."

Her hand in his again, he pulled it close and kissed it once, then walked away.

"You look to be having a great time, My Lady."

'I am, thank you. How about you, Demarko, enjoying yourself?"

"I am—"

A tight grip on her arm pulled her attention away from Demarko. Turning to look behind her, she saw it was Slaine who held her arm dragging her away. Pain seared all the way down to the bone and attempting to pull away only made the pain worse. Not wanting to cause a scene, she quickened her steps where she walked beside him hoping no one would look too close. *I knew it! He is always acting like a brute.*

Her feet stopped moving, his grip loosened, and she stared at the man leaning on the wall. She watched out of the corner of her eye the man next to her. Keeping her voice low, but stern, she questioned them about their actions.

"What is going on? Why have you literally dragged me all the way over here?"

"Because I want to talk you."

"All you had to do was ask, no need for the theatrics."

"What were you doing?"

"It looked to me like she was doing what you *asked* her not to."

Rolling her eyes at him, she turned and looked at Slaine, determined to ignore Deklan.

"Is that what this is about…because I danced with Kip?"

"I did ask you not to."

"He's one of our Elite Guards who's loyal to us. It was just a dance. It's not as if we plotted to run away together."

"From here, it looked as if you and Demarko were getting quite close."

Balling her hands into fists, she turned to Deklan and snapped at him.

"Would you butt out? Why don't you go find something to play with in that tower of yours!"

Turning her attention back to Slaine, she said, "I'm going to find Arabella. I will talk to you later when you have calmed down and you have one less brother attached to you."

Facing the crowd and with her back toward her aggravation, she heard his snide comment.

"Why would you waste your time visiting with the help? They are beneath you! What could she offer you, but as your servant? That is all she is good for. Servants have no business dealing with royalty except to do as they are told."

She stopped, her body trembled, and her fury peaked. With tunnel vision and almost blinded by rage, she turned and pointed her finger at Deklan, unleashing her anger. "What did you just say?"

"I said—"

"I heard what you said. I just wanted to see if you meant it the way it sounded. By the smug look on your face, you did. She is not a servant! None of these people *are* servants! The town's people are friends, not low life nobodies. Arabella is my friend and has more to offer than you ever could."

"Blaze, that'll be quite enough. We will talk about this somewhere else."

Jerking out if his hold, she glared at him, but didn't follow his orders.

"No! He will hear what I have to say! I have had enough of his antics and rude comments. If either of you don't like it, too bad!"

Taking two steps closer to Deklan, she began where she left off, her voice getting louder and louder with each word that passed her lips.

"You arrogance makes me sick. The bile that pours out of your mouth is insulting to say the least. I can't believe after you have been invited into our home and cared for, you would insult the very people who were gracious enough to allow you entry. I won't stand for that behavior anymore! I don't care who you think you are, but you will be respectful to everyone. If you don't, I will have you locked up in the deepest darkest dungeon hole I can find and refuse to let anyone care for, or feed you! Is that understood, Deklan?"

Inhaling two deep breaths, she pulled her anger back and waited for an answer. "Yes or no? I'm running out of the small amount of patience I have left."

Her body slammed into the wall and slid to the ground. Slaine's angry voice screamed in her ears while his face filled her vision, red-rimmed eyes on fire.

"How dare you speak to him in such a manner. He's my brother and he's right! I won't tolerate you embarrassing him in front of all of these people. I would never allow him to do that to you."

Her arm in his grip again, her body jerked from the floor and forced to face Deklan.

"You'll apologize and you'll do it now. You screamed at him in front of an audience, now you make it right in front of *your* audience."

Her fists were balls of fury and her body shook from anger. Her heart hammered in her ears and the taste of blood lingered on her tongue. She did the nicest thing she could do. Looking from one face to another, their expressions matched smug and superior. Spitting the blood out of her mouth, she smiled at both of them, waited a half a second, then turned and walked away. Working her way through the crowd, their sorrow floated into her ears and soft hands caressed her cheeks and back as she continued until she shut the doors behind her, blocking it all out.

* * * *

I would like to rip their throats out! How dare they treat her so badly! Flexing his muscles, Demarko felt the rage running through his veins. He welcomed it, relished in it. His body tight, his pulse racing, his frenzied fury deafened the sound of his heart shattering like broken glass. Watching her, he felt proud, then afraid, and by the time she ran by, he felt gut wrenching pain from the tears in her eyes. He felt more than anger—disgust filled his entire being. *She was so hurt. They deserve to die, or at least be beaten half to death, brought back and beaten again. I have to get out of here. Now is not the time and here is not the place.*

Willing his feet to move, he walked stiffly out the main doors through the entrance hall and into the crisp night air. Bent half over, hands on his knees, he breathed deeply as he tried to quell his rage. Someone grabbed his shoulder. Standing up, a fisted hand pulled back ready to swing, he stopped when Shaunt's voice sounded in his ears.

"Easy now! Let's go for a walk before you end up on the chopping block."

"They would have to subdue me first. I bet I can pummel them both into the dirt without receiving so much as a scratch. "

"You are probably right, but they won't be the ones coming after you. It will be a handful of his nasty guards. Now, move!"

He dropped his hand and followed the old man. "Fine. Did you see her face, how much pain, she was in?"

"Yes, Son, I did. It was a gruesome display."

"She had tears streaming down her face like a hard rain upon a window, in uncontrollable streams. I have never seen anyone cry like that. It's heartbreaking. What are we going to do?"

"Right now, we are going to the garden so you can calm down."

"I think I know what happened to us."

"You do?"

"Yes, I think she ran away because of this kind of behavior. I'm certain that if she asked, I would go with her again."

"That is a nice story, but that's not what happened."

"Then what happened?"

"Um, well… Let's not worry about that now. We need to get you in the garden before they come looking for you."

"Good. Let them! As angry as I am, they are probably going to need a handful of guards just to take me." Walking toward the garden next to Shaunt, he stopped when they reached the gate.

"Are we going to climb over? Let me restate that—do you need me to toss *you* over?"

"Oh, first, you are ready to kill and now you are cracking jokes. No, thank you. I have a key."

"I have to do something to keep me from turning around and giving them what they deserve. His hands should be severed and fed to the pigs, for touching her like that."

"No, you need to stop thinking that way. You won't be helping Blaze that way. It'll only make things worse for her."

His body froze, his chest tightened and his breathing stopped. Heart in his throat, he tried to swallow back the realization of those words. Choking them back, he gulped for air and finally spoke. "I'm sorry. I didn't think about that. You're right! Well, only if I don't succeed at grinding them to dust. Nevertheless, he would blame her and she would be in more danger than she already is. I have to admit, most of my fury is from what I fear they may do next since she so publicly humiliated him. He deserved it. But I still fear for her."

"Here, follow me. There is a bench just over there where we can sit and talk."

"Why does he have to be so hateful to her? She is such a wonderful person. If she were my wife, I would break any hand in anger that came at her. She would never have to wonder if I loved her. She would always be able to see it. Shaunt, I'm confused about how I feel. I know I love her. I feel how much I love her. She is my Queen, but I think I'm *in love* with her. How can that be? I'm not sure what it is or what's proper to feel. I won't interfere and make things worse even though it angers me."

He turned his body toward the bench and noticed Shaunt's movements. His eyes were closed, his lips barely moved and his hands moved in small patterns around the two of them. As he sat on the bench and leaned back, he stared at the old man. Shaunt suddenly stopped and dropped his hands.

"What are you doing?"

"Nothing. Follow your heart!"

"Shaunt, I just told you, I think my heart is confused. I can't be in love with her. She belongs to someone else."

"No. Your mind is confused and it will lead you in the wrong direction. Trust only your heart. I know things are crazy right now and you don't understand. Try not to worry. Things will work out. Your mind will mend and your memory will return. I know you are confused and are unsure about your feelings, but be patient. As I said, follow your heart and your instincts. They will lead you in the direction of truth."

How is my heart going to lead me to the truth when I have no idea what the truth is. My mind is boggled and my heart is confused. I guess that means I will roam aimlessly until my memories return and my life is put back together.

"Shaunt—"

"Sit back, relax, and let your body and mind calm. Clear your mind of all its clutter. Let me know when you are calm and collected."

Scooting down a little, back against the wooden bench, he tilted his head back and rested it on the seat, coaxing his mind to peace. Hands folded on top of his chest, he took a few deep breaths, and Shaunt's muttered words flowed into his ears. Body feeling heavy, he tried to lift his head to ask a question only to fall short and fall asleep. *His* wedding day played behind his eyes...

Chapter Eleven
Fact or Fiction?

Dried tears stuck to her cheeks and her eyes were puffy and red, but, she had finally cried out her anger and frustration. Her muscles ached, her chest was on fire and her body felt drained. Closing her eyes, she inhaled, focusing on the aroma of flowers and steam in the air. *This is why this is my favorite place. So peaceful and relaxing.* Wiggling her toes in the cool grass and opening her eyes, she stood watching the water as it fell and collected in the spring. *Even at night, this garden is so beautiful, so full of life. It's almost magical. I swear that lily and star are alive.* Lifting the hem of her dress, she walked over and placed her feet in the shallow part of the spring. She moved her left foot in an arc shape and stared at the ripples dancing across the surface. A worried voice from behind, spooked her.

"Blaze, we have been looking for you."

Putting weight back on both feet, she turned around to see Arabella and Shaunt standing there.

"Sorry. I was in one of the guest rooms for a while and then decided to come down here. I love it here. It's so peaceful."

Movement out of the corner of her eye caught her attention. Shaunt moved in front of Arabella. His hands racked through his hair, looking clearly disturbed and his eyes lit up with an enraged fire as he spoke "It's time, Arabella. I'm not sure how much more these two can take. For that matter, I'm not sure how much we can take. This has gone on long enough. "

"I agree with all of it. You are right. It's time and I, too am not sure how much more the two of them can take."

Her brows furrowed as confusion crossed her face. "Who? What two and what can't they take? What are *you* two talking about?"

Her frame, pulled into a brief hug by the man, she watched, still confused as Shaunt stormed out of the garden. She quickly turned to her friend.

"What's going on?"

"We need to talk. Come and sit with me a spell and I will explain it to you."

She followed behind the woman and sat down. Once seated, she turned a questioning look Arabella's way.

"Arabella, you and Shaunt are starting to scare me. Would you please tell me what's going on?"

"You *should* be scared. It's a horrifying tale. Once the truth is revealed, you and Demarko will never be the same…"

About the Author

Creativity is my addiction and writing is my drug of choice! Midwest living, wife and mother, who loves to read, write, and listen to Rock music. I have a vivid imagination that runs wild and on its own tangents at times.

www.ingramcontent.com/pod-product-compliance
Lightning Source LLC
Chambersburg PA
CBHW052138170626
46812CB00004B/1488